Slightly Spooky Stories V

Patsy Collins

The author can be found at
www.patsycollins.co.uk

ISBN: 978-1-914339-48-6

Contents

1. Lover's Leap

"Why do you think it's called Lover's Leap?" Michael had asked a year ago.

"Maybe, because it's such a romantic looking spot, this is where lots of people get engaged. Take that leap into the unknown?" Lauren suggested.

"Like you have with me?"

She'd laughed. "I didn't leap, I was pushed!"

"In the right direction though?"

"Oh yes, very much so." She'd then thrown a few of the flowers, saved from her bouquet, so the breeze carried them out to sea. "So our love will always be here," Lauren had said. "It'll wash in on every tide."

"Then we'd better come back every year."

"I'd like that."

Now, one year on, she stood in the same spot. Below her on the beach children ran squealing into the waves, lovers strolled hand in hand, dads queued for ice cream. As Lauren watched, a couple drew a love heart in the damp sand and put their initials inside. They stepped away, onto a dry part of the beach and kissed as they sea washed away their handiwork.

"That's about right!" Although she was alone on the clifftop, Lauren spoke the words aloud.

They'd come here on honeymoon, Lauren and Michael. Back then Lauren thought she had everything she could ever want. A man she loved, who loved her in return and would never leave her. A wonderful family in the form of his three children. A small but cosy home to keep them all safe. She'd been right.

"It's all gone!" she wailed.

"What has?" The voice was gentle. Kind.

"I thought I was by myself up here," Lauren said to the young woman wearing a pretty, retro-looking print dress.

"No one is alone on Lover's Leap."

Lauren was. Michael hadn't left her, he'd been taken from her. Another driver sending a text to say they were running late had swerved and made themselves later still. Michael didn't make it home ever again. The children had gone back to their mother. Lauren's safe home felt like a prison.

"It's all such a waste," Lauren said.

"What is?" the woman asked gently.

Lauren spoke about the lovers drawing on the beach and the tide washing away the image, but she meant the lost time with Michael. The six years she'd refused to marry him for fear their marriage would end like his first.

"Alexia and I just weren't right for each other. She'll tell you the same. I wanted children and stability, she wanted freedom and adventure," Michael had explained.

Then one day she'd asked his twin girls what they'd most like to do in the school holidays.

"Be your bridesmaids," they'd instantly replied in unison.

"Mum said we can stay with her for a week so you can go on honeymoon," Lucy had added.

So they'd married and afterwards come to Lover's Leap. They hadn't stayed actually on the cliff, but had walked up there along the coastal path every day. Sometimes they continued on for miles, enjoying the countryside full of birdsong and wild flowers. Other days they climbed down to the beach, stretched out in the hot sun and made plans.

"It's still there," the lady said. It was odd how Lauren only noticed the woman in the floral dress was beside her when she spoke, yet lost as she was in her own thoughts, the stranger's voice didn't startle her.

"What's still there?" Lauren asked.

"The love. It's still in the water, don't you think?"

This time Lauren was taken aback by her words. How could this woman know about the flowers she'd thrown?

"People express their love in words up here, or down on the beach with messages in the sand. The tide takes them out to sea, but the love is never really gone. It stays in the water, to be washed ashore time after time."

Ah. She was talking about the heart and initials Lauren said she'd seen get wiped away. "They won't be there if that happens. They'll have gone home." Or gone forever like Michael.

"You're right. The tide won't wait for them, but will wash that love ashore for others. It will spread it over lovers, friends, families. Different kinds of love, in different places, yet still always the same. Always here for those who come looking for it."

As the woman spoke, Lauren realised the words were true, for her at least. "Thank you," she said, but once again she was alone. The woman in the floral dress was walking back down the coastal path, side by side with a young man. It looked as though she'd found her love.

Lauren knew where she could find love of a different kind. She rang Alexia. "How are the girls?"

"They're fine, but missing you." And no doubt driving their mother to distraction. Alexia did love the three of them, but had got used to having her freedom during the years since her divorce from Micheal. She'd made it clear that losing their father didn't mean Lauren had to lose her relationship with his children.

"I'll come and get them. Can you ask them to pack things for the beach?"

"No problem. See you soon!"

The following day children squealed as they dipped their toes into rock pools, families strolled along the water's edge, a stepmother joined the queue for ice cream.

"Do you know why it's called Lover's Leap?" asked Sammie.

"Your dad asked me that."

"So you know the story?"

"No, we just guessed."

"I know! There was this couple who had a massive row. The woman, thinking he didn't love her anymore jumped off the cliff and died."

"That's so sad," her sister Lucy said.

"But romantic too, because he realised he couldn't live without her and jumped in too, so they would always be together and their love would always be in the water."

"It is," Lauren said. "I'm sure it is." And maybe the couple too were always there, always guiding people away from sadness and towards the love.

2. Comfort Food

On the day Martha heard her brother was dead she began preparations to bake a cake. She wasn't celebrating, not exactly. It was comfort food in every sense of the word. The comfort of making it as she dealt with the difficult emotions his death brought. She could put behind her all the hurt he'd caused, and the fear she'd never escape him. She could look forward to the future. A life without his taunts and little cruelties, and with the cake to eat. A pleasure he couldn't take away from her. Not now.

The police didn't just inform, but questioned her too. It was OK though. For one thing, she'd had an alibi of sorts. The lady in the hardware store recalled she'd been in that day, looking at the new range of baking equipment. She remembered because the moment Martha learned the news, she went back to buy the largest of the square tins.

"I nearly bought this when I was here earlier," she said, almost truthfully. She'd wanted one just like it, but her brother would have questioned the expense, made her pay one way or another. Martha explained it would bring comfort, after the shocking news she'd just received.

"Oh, honey I'm that sorry," the storekeeper said. She still charged full price, but that no longer mattered.

Establishing she'd been elsewhere when her brother fell hardly mattered either. He hadn't been pushed, as far as anybody knew. If the incident had been witnessed, he wouldn't have lain alone in the courtyard until his skin grew as cold as his heart.

Once she had her tin, Martha bought the ingredients she'd need. She already had the basics, but wanted succulent fruit, decadent spices, the sweetest nuts. It would be like Christmas should have been. Would be in future.

As Martha beat together the butter and sugar, she recalled how her brother had blighted her life. Robbing her of hope, spoiling anything nice. It helped her make the batter light. She blended in the eggs and flour. Then the good stuff. Cherries, apricots, cranberries, brazils, ginger, cinnamon… Martha, for the first time ever, had it all.

As the cake cooled, so did her anger. He was gone now. Her suffering was over. She would learn to forget. That night Martha almost took a sleeping pill as usual. There were very few left, but that was another thing which didn't matter. She no longer needed them. There was no-one now to disturb her peace.

Martha was nervous when she cut the first slice of cake. Her brother had spoiled so many little treats of hers. The TV switched off before the end of the show, the piece of pie she'd saved for her lunch taken for his, a greasy stain added to the pretty blouse she found in the charity shop. The last page ripped from books, chemicals put in the water of flowers she'd been given, the chocolates from the bottom layer of the box eaten and replaced with stones. It was hard to believe, even now, that she could have anything nice.

The books and flowers and chocolates, even spoiled as they soon were, had been very rare treats. She'd had to stop using the library once she saw she couldn't return the books undamaged. Boys stopped asking her on dates when they read the messages her brother typed to them on her phone. Typed, showed her, and then either sent or deleted. He'd keep her phone for a while, leaving her with no way to check which. No way to put right any damage he might have done.

He was gone now, he couldn't do anything directly, but he'd still been in her mind as she'd measured and stirred the ingredients. Her painful memories could have caused her to make a mistake. Garlic instead of ginger perhaps, or salt not sugar.

Martha took a tentative bite. The cake was perfect. Rich and sweet. Comforting, just as she'd hoped. She took a proper bite and another. Then paused. Martha set the slice of cake aside while she made coffee. Then she settled into her favourite chair to eat and drink. She could take her time, savour every mouthful. If she wanted to she could eat the whole thing, knowing he wouldn't taunt her that it would make her fat. Fatter. Or snatch it up to eat a big piece in front of her, then put the rest out for the foxes.

After her one slice, Martha put the lid back on the cake tin. It was a lovely thing, sent to the siblings by a Scottish cousin. The embossed and painted lid decorated with a shaggy Highland cow standing amongst heather, against a backdrop of snowy mountains. Inside had been shortbread. Her brother had allowed Martha one buttery finger, just enough for her to know how crumbly and delicious it was. Enough for her to long for more. Then he'd grabbed her wrist, placed her hand over the rim and jammed down the lid.

When he'd released her, she thought her bruised and swollen fingers were all she'd be taking from it. She'd been wrong. He'd given her that beautiful tin once it was empty — to constantly refill with things for him to eat.

From time to time he'd reminded her of that, how he shared things with her. And he always did. Not equally, but enough to keep her tied to him. He wouldn't sell their parents' home and split the money, but he allowed her to keep her childhood bedroom and cook and clean for him. She had no money to buy him out, no job with which to support herself. His little corrections to her school assignments destroyed her academic chances. His constant criticisms ensured she never developed any confidence.

Martha put the cake away, secure in the knowledge that the next day it would be where she'd left it. Day after day she cut another slice, ate it slowly, drawing out the pleasure. Then she closed the lid and returned the tin to the shelf.

At his funeral Martha wept. Tears of relief that it was over. She'd thanked the minister and slipped away from the few mourners, made up of nosy neighbours and some of her bother's colleagues. She'd gone home, her home now, intending to eat the last slice of cake and plan her future.

She brewed coffee, added milk and reached for the cake tin. It was as light as her mood.

Martha prised open the lid and looked in. It was empty. No. No, no, no.

She steadied herself against the kitchen counter. It was OK. She'd just made a mistake. She'd eaten it herself and forgotten. That would be it. She'd been emotional that morning, distracted. Anyone would be before they buried their brother. She told herself that over and over as the coffee cooled and dusk fell.

Then something lit up the scene outside the kitchen window. A fox had triggered the security lights. It slunk onto the grass, poised to sniff at a wedge of something dark. It was Martha's last piece of cake, she had no trace of doubt. She watched as the fox ate every last crumb, and knew she'd never be free.

3. Neighbourhood Witch

Myrtle Craggitt is a good neighbour in a lot of ways. We're never disturbed by noise from her house and she keeps her garden neat. She doesn't go out to work, so is useful for taking in parcels. She doesn't drive, which leaves room for both of our cars on the shared driveway. She put out our bins and watered our hanging baskets while we were on holiday.

Are you expecting a but? We were from the way Mr and Mrs Smith, the people we bought the house from, spoke about her.

"It's a quiet, trouble free street," Mrs Smith said. She pointed in the direction of Myrtle's half of the property. "The neighbourhood watch sees to that."

At least, at the time that's what I assumed she'd said.

When we asked if there had ever been any disagreements over the boundary fence or anything like that, they were rather too eager to assure us that wasn't the case.

"Myrtle Craggitt is very helpful," Mr Smith said. "Very neighbourly."

I took that to mean a bit pushy. Nosy even.

Janice, my wife, agreed that's how it sounded, and thought maybe she was a bit lonely and so eager for company. "If we talk to her, perhaps have her round for coffee, I'm sure we'll soon make friends."

We both thought the Smiths were pushy and desperate when they insisted the sale had to go through before the end of October. We'd have happily complied if we could. We were eager to move from our noisy flat into somewhere with a garden, and taking the kids trick or treating in the street would have been a nice way to get to know our new neighbours. We simply couldn't though. There was a chain preventing our buyers from moving until very early in November.

The Smiths decided to move out anyway and left the house empty for five days. When we heard they were going to do that, we called on Myrtle, explained the house wouldn't be empty for long and left our phone number, 'just in case'.

"Thank you for letting me know," she said. "I'm sure you'll all be happy living here."

We hadn't mentioned the kids, but we'd brought them on a viewing. She must have seen and remembered that. It was a comfort to know there was an observant neighbour keeping her eye on the place. We moved in two days before bonfire night and piled some of the boxes we'd used for moving, and some bits of rotten wood we discovered in the garden, intending to burn it.

Myrtle appeared. "I do not like fireworks. They are dangerous and scare animals." She spoke softly, but her tone, expression and posture all implied, 'And therefore you won't have any'.

I'm a young man and almost two feet taller than our neighbour, so I won't say I felt intimidated, but I had the distinct impression she expected her opinion to be the last word on the subject. To show I wasn't prepared to be bullied, I said, "I happen to like them." And then because I didn't want an unnecessary argument, and it was true, I also agreed with her that having them at home wasn't wise. "We're going to a proper display at the race course."

Myrtle nodded and it felt as though I'd passed a test.

"I'm Paul," I informed her, wanting to be friendly. "I work in the bank in town. My wife Janice is a hairdresser. She's walking Tish and Joe back from school. Luckily the move didn't mean they had to change."

"Myrtle Craggitt. Don't trust banks and never have my hair cut. I like children though." She gave a peculiar smile, then walked away. An extremely long plait hung down her back.

Myrtle returned just after Janice and the kids came home. "Gingerbread," she announced, holding out a heaped plate of the stuff. "Learning makes you hungry. Have you been learning?"

Tish and Joe assured her they had and proved it with random facts and a mini spelling bee. The gingerbread was ridiculously delicious.

Later Janice told me Myrtle often plied the children with cookies and cakes after school. "It's making them try really hard in class, so they can impress her with good marks."

"That's good, but…"

"I saved you a treacle cookie."

All thoughts of suggesting we try to dissuade Myrtle from feeding the children so much sugar and carbs vanished at the first bite.

"She obviously loves kids and as ours are the only ones in the street, I suppose it's natural she makes a fuss of them," Janice said.

"It's odd that, isn't it? All these houses big enough for families and no children."

Unsurprisingly the kids took a bit of a shine to Myrtle and were always chatting to her over the fence. The baked goods helped obviously. So did her cat Blackberry. A huge bundle of fluff which was willing to be picked up, cuddled and stroked, but only appeared when his mistress did. Mostly though it was because the kids were at the asking questions stage.

One day, after they'd been at it for over an hour, and knowing how tiring the constant 'why?' can be, I apologised to Myrtle.

"It's good for them to be interested in things and I can always disappear when I've had enough."

Myrtle somehow seemed to know things, and not just answers to the kids' varied questions. I'm sure we never actually told her about our holiday, but she offered to keep an eye on the place while we were away.

"If you could put out the bin, that would be helpful," I said. "It shouldn't be heavy."

I didn't mention the hanging baskets, but they were a cascade of health and colour when we returned.

"I couldn't bear to see the poor things suffer," she said when I thanked her. It made me feel ashamed of the way I usually forgot to water them until they were wilted and sad looking. I made a better job of their care after that.

Really the only snag with Myrtle Craggitt was that she was so serious, a bit intense. When the kids were invited to a fancy dress party they asked to borrow her hat as they were going as pirates. Quite a lecture we all got about how pirates aren't cartoon characters or friendly Johnny Depp lookalikes with a code, but real men forced by circumstance to put their lives and those of others at risk.

When Tish lost a tooth, Mrytle must have heard me mention tooth fairies.

She soon put us right by declaring, "There's no such thing. Dentists are real and if you children want to avoid those, you'd better brush properly."

I got a telling off for not telling them the truth. Even so I'm grateful. They've not had a filling since and I've not had to get up in the night to leave coins under pillows.

Coming up to Christmas she expressed her thoughts on the 'Santa stop here' sign. The children weren't close enough to hear, and Janice and I decided against taking Myrtle's advice to tell them Father Christmas didn't exist. We did however decide to spend a little less on their gifts and both be at home on Saturdays, instead of taking turns to work overtime.

This year Myrtle's lightened up quite a lot. At Easter she was pleased to know Tish and Joe didn't believe in an Easter bunny, but were fans of chocolate.

"If you have a stepladder you could tie it to mine and make a bridge over the fence, so there's more room for your egg hunt without all the little ones going out in the street."

Luckily we had decided to organise a hunt for our kids and their cousins, so her words didn't raise expectations we weren't ready to meet. The haul of goodies they brought back was considerably larger than we'd put out. The kids brushed their teeth after eating some.

Over summer she let the kids camp out on her lawn, watered our plants when we were away and was just as helpful and neighbourly as the Smiths had promised the year before. Come the end of October though, I was reminded of how insincere they'd sounded as they said it, and of their insistence on being out by the end of the month.

Myrtle decorated her home for hallowe'en. There were bats dangling from her trees and guttering, mounds of glowing pumpkins, and glistening, ghostly cobwebs everywhere. We didn't see her do it, but we weren't looking. She dressed herself up too. Her big black hat was on her head and a black cloak was around her shoulders. Blackberry wound himself around her booted ankles.

All Myrtle's electric lights were switched off and the place lit with candles. They cast eerie shadows and made her nose look much bigger than before. I hadn't noticed those warts either. Who'd have thought she'd be so good with makeup?

When the kids called 'trick or treat!' she laughed. I'd never heard her do that before – no way would I have forgotten that cackle.

"You wouldn't play a trick on me, would you?" she asked.

The kids assured her they wouldn't. "We've brought you a treat!" They produced a slice of the pumpkin pie we'd made from the bits we carved out to make room for the tea-light and spooky face.

"Treats all round then," she said. "Who wants to go flying?"

I was about to remind her of the importance of always telling the truth, but was drowned out by Tish and Joe's squeals of delight. Myrtle's broom glided out of the house and hovered at just the right height for them to climb onboard.

4. Taking My Own Advice

My friends and family were always giving me advice, all of it well meant. I could easily see why they thought I needed help. Give me a sketch pad or knitting needles and I know what I'm doing, but expect me to interact with the real world and I'm lost. Not only that, but I was unfit, overweight and had messy hair. I did have a great personality though. My friends assured me of that and I guessed it was the reason they were so keen to help.

A colleague told me about the power of attraction. "You have to imagine yourself having or doing whatever it is," she said.

Her life seemed pretty good and she was so enthusiastic I wondered if there could be anything in it.

"No way," my sister said when I explained the key points to her. "You've gotta get up and actually do something not just think about it."

That made sense. I did think, mostly about all the things which could go wrong, so didn't do anything much towards making my dreams come true.

"You're wasting your talent, Fiona," my sister said. "You should get yourself out of that dead end job and take a chance on a career."

"I think you're being sensible keeping your job," my oldest friend told me. "This way you know you can pay the bills and still do your design work in the evenings."

Trouble was, work was tiring. Add that to my uncertainties about the direction my life should take and perhaps you'll understand why a lot of my free time was spent in front of the TV eating pizza instead of drawing and knitting up samples.

"I'm fat," I complained to Mum.

"Nonsense, love. You look better for having a few curves." It was nice of her to say it, but I wasn't convinced.

A magazine article suggested sticking a picture of me looking slim and gorgeous on the fridge and looking at that before opening the door. I didn't have such an image. A piece in the paper suggested doing the same thing with an unflattering picture. I had an excellent one of those, taken after I'd had a bad reaction to a bee sting, and put it to use.

My sister took it down. "You don't want that depressing you. If you're really worried about your weight then join an exercise class or something."

Although it was all kindly meant, and much of it good, the conflicting advice meant I gave up totally. I gave notice at work and announced I was moving away from Mum's. Someone said a fresh start would do me good, but that's not why. Someone else said that if I was going to make big changes in my life I'd need the security of familiar surroundings. I just wanted to escape all the well intentioned advice and try to make some decisions for myself.

A visit to the estate agent showed me the only place I could afford to rent was a caravan. At first I wasn't sure, but I eventually decided I rather liked that idea. If I'd been offered something built from bricks and looking permanent I may have chickened out. Staying in a caravan sounded more like taking a holiday. I could cope with that.

"Sorry, it's only just become available so we don't have any photos or printed information, but you're welcome to go and take a look before you decide." The estate agent reeled off the details and directions then made a call to the owner to say I'd come for a viewing. "If you decide to take it you can move in straight away. Actually I'd advise you to do just that. As you've seen there's not much else in your price range and it's likely to be snapped up pretty soon."

More advice, but he was just doing his job.

There was a heavy shower as I drove towards the farm where the caravan was located, which made visibility poor. I was just wondering if I'd taken a wrong turning somewhere when I spotted a flash of headlights in one of those convex reflectors people put up to help them get safely out of driveways located on bends. As I slowed to a crawl I caught a glimpse of a girl pulling out of a track. Her car, like mine, was piled with bags and boxes. The previous tenant I assumed. Without thinking I raised a hand in greeting. She returned the gesture and gave a grin as though to acknowledge I was taking her place. Then I turned down where the overgrown sign indicated Long Meadow Farm.

"Mr Davies?" I asked a man with a lamb under his arm. It seemed an odd way to meet a prospective tenant but those gangly legs and curly hair were very appealing. The lamb was kind of cute too.

"I'm David Williams," he told me.

"Oh… sorry. I'm Fiona Jones, come to look at your caravan."

"You are? Right. OK. I'll be right with you." He went into the house and came out with a key and no little sheep. I hoped it wasn't in the oven.

It wasn't one of those big mobile home things the Americans call trailers, which is what I'd been expecting, but a two wheeled caravan designed to be towed behind a car. A Morris Minor by the look of it. That thing was old. The rent though, when he mentioned it, was much less than I'd thought. I realised what had happened; in order to stop hearing conflicting advice I'd stopped listening to anyone properly.

Two things convinced me to accept. One was the girl driving away as I approached. I'd only seen her indistinctly, but there had been something optimistic about her. She was around my age and seemed to be everything I'd like to be. Happy, healthy, attractive. The second was the farmer who'd be my landlord. He was broad of shoulder and slim of hip, but it wasn't so much his nice looks as his gentle manner when I'd dithered about accepting.

"I don't know," I'd admitted. It seemed such a big step. Some of my friends would say it was a great idea, some that it was terrible.

David had just shrugged. "It's entirely up to you." He handed me the keys. "Have a look round on your own and let me know when you've decided."

That startled me. It would have been in his interests to encourage me to say yes, or even to say no, straight away, so he could offer it to someone else. Here, it seemed, was the perfect place to avoid advice.

When I returned to his farmhouse to say I'd take it, I saw the lamb really was in the oven! Or rather the plate warmer part of one of those big range things and it was wrapped in a blanket and the door was open.

"It got chilled," David explained. "Once it's warmed up a bit I'll give it a bottle. Few hours time it should be strong enough to go back to its mother."

I hoped, but didn't say, I was going to be strong enough to cope without mine.

David helped me unload my boxes. He simply carried a few of the biggest and dumped them inside. "No idea where you're going to fit all this lot."

Definitely my landlord wouldn't be a source of unasked for advice.

"You fill the water tank here," he indicated a filler cap on the side of the van. "There's a hose in the barn which will reach." He showed me how to connect up the gas bottle and promised to bring me a spare, then left me alone.

I started on the unpacking, then made myself a cup of tea. As I hunted for biscuits my landlord went past with the lamb tucked inside his jacket.

"Is it going to be OK?" I called through my window.

"Come with me and see, if you like."

I abandoned my tea and scrambled into boots and one of my handmade cardigans. We walked and walked and walked. The other sheep were making quite a racket and soon the lamb was bleating too. I knew nothing about sheep but even I could tell from the way the lamb bounded towards its mum and started drinking that it was feeling better than when I'd seen it earlier.

Another sheep was about to give birth, David thought. "Are you in a rush to get back?" he asked.

I'd have said I wasn't even if I really had something interesting to get back for. While we waited I helped David shaking out clean straw for a whole flock of sheep to sleep on, and filling troughs with water. The expectant ewe gave birth to twins; a slightly icky but totally fascinating process.

Altogether it was a long, tiring day, emotionally and physically. Without bothering to finish unpacking I fell into bed exhausted and slept soundly. In the morning I felt far more positive than I had in a long while. The only food I could find was the fruit basket one friend from work had given me as a leaving present. I ate some of that and dressed in the first clothes I could find, which were sports ones I'd bought in a sale and never put to their intended use.

Walking to the village shops seemed a good idea. It didn't take me long to become breathless and I had no doubt my face was glowing. Then, as I walked past the tiny car dealership, I saw her again. The girl I'd seen as I looked for the farm. One minute she was right opposite, the next she'd vanished. I'd only looked away for a moment to stop myself staring, so she must have gone into one of the row of pretty cottages she'd been walking past.

Suddenly I wanted her to have a good opinion of me. I couldn't just think myself thin, I knew because I'd tried that countless times, usually whilst crunching my way through a packet of biscuits. I couldn't instantly give my hair any kind of style, but I could tidy it up by pulling it into a ponytail and securing it with one of the oddments of yarn which collect in all my pockets. I couldn't make myself look less exhausted either but I could present that in a better light, by making it seem I was jogging, so I ran past the cottages. Fortunately there was a bend in the road just after, so I could stop before I crashed with exhaustion.

I couldn't buy much because of having to carry it and I had to take the long way back so the girl wouldn't know I'd been running to get food, not fit. That meant sticking to the essentials and going without junk.

Work on my designs took up all the limited space so it was easier to have fruit and water for lunch than cook a meal. There was no TV, or anything else to do when I wasn't working or sleeping so I started going for walks. I collected small pieces of fleece snagged on bushes and wire fences, wondering if I could learn to spin. The colours and contours of the land inspired my designs.

Occasionally, when I went into the village, I was asked about whatever item of knitwear I was wearing. It seemed there might be a demand for something unique which had been handmade locally. David too was interested in my work, both what I produced and where I bought the wool. He seemed delighted with the thick sweater I created for him.

David's fields and hilly woodland were wrapped around the space where his house and my caravan stood, so it wasn't surprising that I often encountered him. I usually stopped to chat or help him with what he was doing. OK, I admit I made sure I saw him every day and indulged in the occasional fantasy about life as a farmer's wife.

Having told everyone I knew that I wanted a complete break for a while meant I rarely saw anyone else. Perhaps because of that I found myself wondering about the mystery girl I'd glimpsed. We'd not exchanged a word and I knew nothing about her, but as she apparently lived locally it was likely we'd meet again. I hoped so, and that when it happened she'd form a good opinion of me. Remembering how I'd jogged along the High Street in an attempt to give her the idea I was fit, I put more effort into my walks –

increasing both the speed and distance. I was encouraged by my rate of progress.

On my return I met David and asked about the girl who'd rented the caravan before I'd moved in.

"It was empty before you came. It seemed odd you wanting to live in it but I thought it'd be nice to have someone living close by and at least it shut everyone up."

"What are you talking about?" I asked, puzzled. "The estate agent sent me here because you told him your previous tenant was just about to leave."

"No, I… oh, you're not confusing me with Sam Davies at Long Meadow Farm are you? His place and Little Meadow often get mixed up and he's got one of those big mobile home things he rents out."

"Oh dear, that sounds right."

I went back to estate agents to apologise. On my way out I pushed back the undergrowth from the sign so no one else would see an L, bunch of greenery and 'Meadow Farm' and make the same mistake I had. The estate agent was very nice about my not going to the viewing he'd arranged and not contacting him. He said that kind of thing often happened, which actually made me feel worse.

On the way back I started to wonder what David had meant by shutting people up. If he was in the farmyard when I got back I'd ask him, I decided. That's not as brave as it sounds as generally he was out in the fields at that time of day. Not that day though. He seemed happy to explain, almost as though he'd been waiting for me to ask.

"Someone said the caravan was an eyesore and I should get rid of it. Someone else said it was antique and I should restore it."

"So you decided to rent it out?"

"No. I'd cleaned it up a bit but hadn't made a decision when you arrived. You seemed so sure of what you wanted and well… it seemed a good idea." He actually blushed.

"And you thought it might be nice to have some company?"

"Yes."

"But only after I arrived wanting somewhere to stay?"

"Er… yes."

Now you're probably quicker on the uptake than me when it comes to romance and had seen this coming, but with me it took a while for it to sink in. It took even longer for me to do anything about it. Anything sensible that is. I was very quick to mumble incoherently and run and hide in the caravan. Once there, it hit me pretty quickly that David liked me and that I really, really liked him and would be more than happy to provide him with as much company as he wanted. It also occurred to me that if he considered me decisive then he definitely wasn't. That meant I was going to have to be the one to make the first move.

In order to give me some confidence I decided to have my hair done.

The stylist wore a badge saying 'Kiri'. She helped me into a gown and offered me a seat in front of a steamed up mirror.

"What would you like done?"

I had no idea of course, which was why my hair was so messy. "What do you advise?" I asked, which made me smile. For years I'd been getting unasked for advice, now I was actually asking. It felt like a positive step.

Kiri washed my hair, then began to snip. For what seemed like hours she had my hair combed over my eyes or had me lift my head so I was studying the chandeliers, or dropping it to stare at my knees, and then she stood in front of me with the huge diffuser blocking my view.

Eventually she finished and stood aside. "What do you think?"

I saw the girl again. Not a glimpse in passing but right in front of me meeting my gaze… in the mirror.

"I'm her! She's me!"

"Uh, is that good?" Kiri asked.

"Yes. Yes, it is. I don't know what's happened but you've made me look like the person I wanted to be."

It had stopped raining by then so I was able to walk back without spoiling my new hairstyle. As I drew level to the cottages I looked around and saw my reflection in the glass front of the car dealership. The way I was rushing along before, with my hair in my eyes, had meant I hadn't properly seen what I was looking at – myself. It was all clear to me then. When I'd seen a car just like mine apparently pulling out of the farm track I'd really only seen my own reflection, in the mirror opposite the farm track. My mind had reflected back the image of the person I'd wanted to be. Thanks both to that, and doing something about it, I'd become the happy, decisive woman David thought he'd seen when I arrived in his farmyard. By the time I'd worked all that out I was back there again knocking on his door.

It took a lot longer for me to move out of the caravan and into the farmhouse. I got lots of advice about that from my family and friends. At first the advice was conflicting but once those people close to me had met David and got a good look at the new happier, fitter, more confident me they all said the same thing; "Go for it."

This was a year ago. I'm now Mrs David Williams and between us we're launching a new line of knitwear designed by me, knitted by the new friends I've made in the village, and using wool from Little Meadow sheep.

5. Seeking Salvation

Nobody ever did anything to help her. In the dreary town where she'd been born, she'd received nothing but disapproval. If she could get away things would be better.

"You can't run away from yourself," Mother had said, then left for church.

Mother spoke in clichés; the girl found the imagination to escape.

She travelled no further than the bottom of a glass. She escaped her home, warmth and food. Each grey morning she awoke; in a doorway, bus station, cardboard box. She couldn't get free.

The state was no help. It begrudgingly doled out enough money to exist. Never enough to live. She'd never really lived. Never would.

"Ask for God's guidance," Mother pleaded. That was no help, the girl didn't believe in Him.

The church thought she'd live on after death. Maybe they were right, who knew? They knew they were right about sin. She'd sinned. Not much, she didn't know how to do more and couldn't afford to find out. The church would forgive her wouldn't it? It'd forgive her if she asked on Sunday.

It was Wednesday. The church would be closed to her. She'd spill her blood on its wide stone steps. They'd see she'd tried the door and, finding the way to sanctuary and salvation blocked. She'd find her own way. Away from trouble, from pain, from forgiveness.

Mother would come to church an extra day next week. Sunday to pray for herself. Again at her daughter's funeral. What would she pray for then? Forgiveness maybe. Can the dead forgive?

She climbed those falsely welcoming steps. She pushed against the door barring her way.

It opened.

6. Little Lost Bear

Was that the doorbell? It had rung so infrequently recently she might be forgiven for forgetting what it sounded like.

Melanie had been so lonely since Anne died. The girls had been friends since secondary school, their relationship turning to love when they started college. Melanie had often gone with Anne to family functions and always been treated with kindness and affection. When Anne explained to her parents, Linda and Paul, how she felt about Melanie they'd seemed shocked at first, but it wasn't long before she was again welcomed at family events. She was always introduced as, and spoken of, as Anne's friend or flatmate, but that didn't worry her. Until Anne's death, Melanie believed they'd accepted the relationship but preferred not to discuss it. Melanie's own parents weren't accepting at all.

Gary, Anne's brother, was different. He was openly pleased his sister had someone special in her life. He often spent part of his leave with the girls in their tiny terraced home, sent Christmas cards to them as a couple and called Melanie his sister-in-law.

When Anne was killed the shock had been terrible for all of them. The pain hit Melanie as though she too had been struck by a speeding car. Gary helped, soothing her while she sobbed. He held her hand through the funeral and held her together afterwards.

It was only after he left to rejoin his ship Melanie noticed his parents had kept their distance since the funeral. When she rang them Linda spoke politely. When she knocked on the door Paul opened it, but she knew they'd have been happier not to see her. Melanie felt so rejected by them. It seemed she'd lost much more than the woman she loved. She was sad too that she couldn't comfort them. She and Gary had chatted for hours about Anne, each remembering happy times. Often it made them cry, but it helped too.

The doorbell rang again. If she continued ignoring it, would whoever it was go away? Maybe the caller didn't really want her? It could be an important delivery for a neighbour.

Melanie grabbed a towel to wrap round her head so she looked like she'd just had a shower. That would seem to explain why she was still in her PJs and slippers in the middle of the day.

She pulled open the door. There was no one there. As she stepped outside, to see if there was a delivery van in the street, she spotted a small, scruffy teddy bear. It was pale blue with once white paws, and black buttons for eyes. Melanie picked it up and spotted a handwritten note saying, *Please take care of me*. She hugged it.

"Don't worry little bear, I'll look after you."

She took it inside and sat it on the kitchen table. The bear looked thin and unkempt.

"I'm sure you were left for a reason." Melanie scratched her head as she wondered what the reason could be. She felt the towel. Perhaps she should take the shower it was there to represent. It might wake her up a bit and help her figure out about the teddy.

Once dressed, Melanie returned to the kitchen.

"Maybe you belonged to someone as a child and they fell out with their parents but they've brought it round as a peace offering, thinking they still live here?" She switched on the kettle. "Or maybe it's some kind of joke?"

She poured hot water over a teabag and fetched milk. In the fridge were eggs, cheese and mushrooms. She couldn't remember buying them, but they looked OK.

As Melanie cooked and ate she thought up several other ideas about the bear. They all had one thing in common; the bear must have been intended for someone else.

"So the best way I can look after you, little fella, is to find out whose doorstep you should have been left on." One of her neighbours was the obvious choice.

None of the residents of Forton Road recognised the bear, or thought it could be intended for them. It took the rest of the day to discover that, as most of them did more than answer her questions. They said how sorry they were for her loss. They spoke about Anne. Although it brought tears to Melanie's eyes, it was good to hear the nice things they said.

"Will you come in and have a cup of tea?" one grey-haired lady offered.

"I should see about the bear first."

"On your way back then? I'd like to know if he finds a home," Theresa said.

When Melanie returned, saying she'd had no luck, Theresa had a suggestion.

"A couple of times I've had mail for Horton Street, if the postie can make that mistake then perhaps whoever left the bear did the same thing?"

"That's an idea. I'll try there tomorrow."

"Would you mind letting me know how you get on. It's just the bear has reminded me of someone and I'd really like it to find its way home."

It was over a week before Melanie returned. She still had the bear.

"Bad news, I'm afraid." She didn't look as though that were the case. Theresa had been quite shocked at the state of her when she'd called about the bear. She'd got so thin and pale since the girl she'd lived with was killed. Now she had a little colour and didn't seem so listless.

"Come in and tell me about it," Theresa invited.

Melanie explained that she'd tried Horton Street as Theresa had suggested. "No luck for the bear, but the long walk did me good. I slept properly for once. In the morning I remembered a colleague had a child at nursery school so I contacted her to see if she knew of a lost bear. She didn't, but persuaded me to go back to work."

"Oh good. I was rather worried about you."

"'I'm going to be OK." She sipped her tea. "So I've only got the bear to sort out now. I thought I might put his picture on the internet."

"Would that help?"

"It might. People often put pictures up of lost pets, or even people, and they get passed on until someone recognises them."

"I could try that," Theresa said. She wasn't thinking of the bear, but of Alison. Melanie had previously spoken of her sorrow that her parents, and those of Anne, now had very little to do with her. It perhaps wasn't surprising this made Theresa think of her own estranged daughter.

"You use Facebook and all that?" Melanie interrupted her thoughts.

"Not yet. I belong to U3A and they're dragging me up to date. If you don't mind, I'd like to try tracing the bear's owners." If she could learn how to attempt that, she could use the same techniques in search of Alison.

With help from her tutor, Theresa soon had a Facebook page, twitter account and email address. She was surprised how easy it was to master all these things once she had reason to want to. The picture of the bear was soon shared by others in her computer group, then their friends and family. On and on went the photo and her message with it. The one which explained it wasn't only the bear in search of someone they'd lost.

A man got in touch to say he'd sold bears just like that at one time. A lady sent a picture of her own, very similar, bear. It was pleasant to exchange messages with them, even though they didn't provide an answer. Several people contacted her to say she was entitled to lots of money. Her tutor quickly told her what to do about those! Then came the one she'd hardly dared hope for. The one starting, *Hello Mum.*

On her way to the train station, Theresa left a note for Melanie. In it she explained the bear had reminded her of the stuffed toy her daughter had carried everywhere when she was a toddler. It said they'd fallen out some time ago, but the search for the bear had reunited them. *I'm going to stay with her now and meet my granddaughter for the first time. I have the bear with me, but if you trace its owner or want it back quickly for any reason, just let me know and I'll put it in the post.* She left her email address and mobile number.

Two hours later, Alison met Theresa at the station. The first half hour was strained, but gradually they talked more easily. Theresa was pleased her fears had been groundless and Alison was still happily married and seemed to have a good life. She was shocked to learn her granddaughter was twenty years old. She'd missed her whole childhood.

"Did you tell… your husband that you're meeting me?" Theresa asked.

"Yes. He thought it would be best for me to meet you on your own first, rather than for you to come straight to the house."

"A good idea."

'Berhanu suggested we all go out for a meal tonight. Would you like that?"

Theresa nodded. This time she would give the man every chance to show he wasn't any of the awful things she'd said he was.

Over the next few days Theresa looked at hundreds of photos showing her daughter's wedding, Alison pregnant, Alison holding newborn Jasmine, Jasmine on her first day at school, learning to ride a bike and going to the school prom after passing her exams. Alison talked for hours, filling in the details that couldn't be captured on film. Theresa built up an image of a happy, stable family. A family of which she was at last a part.

"You were right to marry him," Theresa said.

Alison placed a hand on her mother's shoulder. "Yes. Yes, I was."

"And I was so very wrong."

"But you're here now. Tell me about that bear."

That discussion was postponed temporarily by first a phone call, then the news that Jasmine was coming over.

It wasn't until two days later when Theresa was packing to go home that she found the bear and told her family all about it.

"He's such a cute little chap," Alison said, "Even if he has seen better days."

"He brings better days, I think," Theresa said.

"I think you're right, Gran. I wonder, could I borrow him?" Jasmine asked.

"If he were mine I'd give him to you, but we don't know whose he is."

Theresa telephoned Melanie. "Would it be all right to pass him on? I shan't be losing touch with my family again, so if you ever traced the owner, I could get him back."

"Yes, do. It seems your granddaughter thinks he can help someone else."

Jasmine, after taking her grandmother to the train station, drove straight over to see Oscar.

"I have something to show you," she said.

"Something you think will get me painting again?"

"No. A mystery." Of course she wanted him to paint again, but if his own talent, the coaxing of gallery owners and critics and pleas of fans couldn't persuade him, then what hope did she have?

"Go on then, show me," Oscar said.

Jasmine took the bear from her shoulder bag and told him all she knew of its history.

"All this time it's been looking for its owner," Oscar said.

"Its quite sad. I mean I know it doesn't really have feelings, but still…"

"I understand what you mean." He empathised with the scruffy little bear. It was on a quest to find its owner and be a much loved companion once again. Oscar wanted back his enthusiasm for art and to cease being an empty shell. People spoke of him as an artist, but he knew differently.

So in tune with those stitched together scraps of fabric and button eyes did he feel, he hardly noticed Jasmine's absence and never questioned her leaving the bear with him. It seemed right for it to hang limply from the corner of his easel.

Jasmine was right, the bear didn't have feelings, but whoever had lost it did. How sad that child must feel. Oscar could almost picture her. It occurred to him he could paint her, that bereft little girl. It had been too long since he'd felt that about anything. He didn't want to do it though. Once he could bring any emotion to life, if misery was all he was left with he'd rather his brushes stayed still.

The image of that child remained in his mind. Nothing he did, not music or drink or sleep could dislodge it. Oscar had experienced such a situation before. It had happened during each of his best pieces of work. He was going to have to paint that child. He still didn't want to, but he knew he must. Perhaps when it was done he'd be able to work again, paint a subject of his choosing.

As Oscar began to sketch the child's outline he mused about the picture he'd really like to do. Not one of misery and loss. One of happiness and love. As he worked on the girl he drew her gazing up longingly to where the bear still dangled. Just out of her reach.

Oscar dropped his pencil as the image in his mind shifted. It was still the same girl, but she didn't look the same. Her arms were outstretched, reaching for the teddy. Such joy on her face! Snatching up the pencil, Oscar worked feverishly. With impatient precision he transferred the picture in his mind onto the canvas and set to work with his paints. When it was done he didn't need anyone to tell him it was good. He knew.

The painting was made into prints. Oscar's return to work caused so much interest they were bought in huge numbers. They were sold in department stores and galleries, hung in homes and businesses.

A print was hanging on the wall of the tea rooms when Linda and Paul walked in. Linda gasped and sank into a chair, more in need of hot, sweet tea than ever.

"What's wrong, love?" Paul asked.

Linda could only point.

Paul looked. "So like our Anne." He too sat down.

"And that bear. It's just like the one she had."

"What can I get you?" the waitress asked.

"A pot of tea and… can we have a closer look at that picture."

"I suppose." She unhooked it from the wall and placed it on the table.

"It isn't her," Linda said. "Similar, but not her."

"No."

"The bear is exactly right though. Do you remember it?"

"Our Gary gave it to her, didn't he? Won it at a fair, I think."

"She carried it everywhere until she was about eleven. That's why it's almost bald round the middle. I had to take it from her when she was asleep so I could wash it."

"And then, when Gary joined the Navy, she gave it to him. She said she knew he'd be safe if he had it with him, because knowing how much she loved it, he'd never let anything happen to it."

"She was such a sweet girl."

"I know, love. I know."

When Gary came home they asked him if he still had the bear.

"No. After the funeral I gave it to Melanie."

"Oh. Her." Linda didn't actually sniff, but her tone suggested it.

"Yes. She loved Anne just like us. She was grieving just like us. Unlike us she was doing it alone. We all had someone who loved Anne to talk to and share our memories with. When I had to go back to sea I knew she wouldn't have anyone. I thought it might help her to at least have something Anne had loved."

"Yes, well…"

"And don't start all that rubbish about her taking Anne away from you. You pushed her away, both of you. Why? You used to like Melanie before you knew the details of their relationship and you know she made Anne happy. If it had been me Melanie loved, not Anne, you'd have welcomed her as a daughter-in-law, wouldn't you?"

Paul nodded.

"That would have been different," Linda stated.

"Not much. Anyway, what does it matter now? You used to have two lovely girls coming round here eating your cakes and making you both laugh. You used to spend days walking along the beach and flying kites with two girls. There used to be two of them here for Sunday lunch, Christmas dinner and to welcome me home. Two of them at birthday parties… That we've all lost Anne is no one's fault. I'm not losing Melanie too. Whether you do is up to you.

I'm going to see her tomorrow. Let me know if you want me to give her a message."

When Melanie opened the door to Gary she hugged him. "Oh, I've missed you!"

"Missed you too, Sis. Is it still OK to call you that? It's how I think about you."

"Of course it is. Come in. I've made you a cake. Not as good as your mum's of course but…"

"I'm guessing you miss her and Dad too."

"Yes. Very much. I'm OK though."

"That's good. You've sounded quite cheerful in your letters but you were such a mess when I saw you last that I've been worried."

"You won't believe it, but it's thanks, in part, to a teddy bear. Someone left it on my doorstep."

"Did it look like this?" He handed Melanie a photo of a pretty little girl holding a bear.

"Yes! Is that Anne?"

"It is. The bear was hers. She gave it to me about the time the two of you met. Just as I was leaving I decided I wanted you to have it. I'd completely forgotten you'd never have seen it before."

"I hadn't. I've not seen a picture of her so young either. Would you let me keep this?"

"It's not mine, it's my parents'. But yes, you can keep it. They thought you might like to have it… and maybe call in sometime and look at some others."

7. Show Me A Sign

"Oh my dear, you look like it's rained on a week's worth of dry washing and that's the least of your troubles." The woman smoothed down her long skirt and sat on the churchyard bench next to Ali. "I'm Adelaide."

Despite herself, Ali found herself smiling at the over-dressed woman and shaking hands with her. "I'm Alison, though most people call me Ali."

Adelaide nodded. "I get called Ali too, sometimes. Now, I feel we're going to be friends so are you going to tell me your worries?"

"I do have something on my mind," she admitted. Why had she said that? Ali didn't often confide in strangers, or anyone else, but she found herself pouring it all out to Adelaide.

Ali's boyfriend wanted to marry her. Nobody but Ali, and Simon himself, seemed to have the slightest doubt she should accept. Simon thought he wasn't good enough for her. Ali thought he was perfect; too perfect.

Ali's son Noah adored Simon and the feeling was mutual. It would be wonderful for Noah to have a proper father and be able to stay on at the village school which he'd been attending since the council moved Ali into Simon's guest house as a temporary measure. She'd later been moved to a flat nearby, but that too was temporary. Without the financial support of someone like Simon, their chances of remaining in the village long term were almost nil.

Simon displayed Ali's artwork in the guesthouse and had sold several pieces for her, which had been a real help. She'd had to stop painting recently, there simply wasn't enough room in the flat to set up her easel or store wet canvasses. If she married Simon she'd have the space to create, Noah could have his own room, and she'd be free from the worry of being moved on. Already in Noah's short life he'd had five different homes.

Ali was really tempted to accept Simon's proposal. But what if she was just saying yes because it was convenient and she didn't really love him? She could break his heart just as hers had been broken when Noah's father took fright and ran from his responsibilities. She needed a sign of some kind to show her if she'd be doing the right thing.

A while back she'd spotted an old car. A vintage Ford Capri, highly polished and obviously cared for, with furry dice hanging from the reversing mirror and the owners' names on the windscreen. One was Simon and the other began with A. When Ali crossed the road to get a proper look, she'd seen it was Amanda. Not her sign then.

Afterwards Ali had gone to the churchyard. She often did on fine days; it was a good place to sketch. Old lichen covered gravestones stood, or lounged in some cases, among wild flowers as the older parts of the churchyard were managed with wildlife conservation in mind. The church too was ancient and picturesque. It was a source of comfort, and shelter from unexpected showers. That's where Ali and Simon would marry. If they married. It was there Adelaide found Ali and persuaded her to talk.

"So you want a sign, do you?"

"Yes," confirmed Ali.

"And you'd believe it if it shared this bench with you, would you?"

Ali twisted round to see if there was a plaque with an inscription, or even a bit of graffiti which seemed to have a message fer her.

"I meant me, you silly goose," Adelaide said. "My husband Simon and I have been happily married for many years and he'll be by my side always."

Despite her old fashioned appearance, Adelaide looked about Ali's age, so could have been married ten years at most. If that felt like 'many years' then maybe she wasn't really as happy as she claimed? Her Simon wasn't within sight either, so there was another exaggeration.

"You're not convinced, and you're right not to be. The kind of sign you're looking for is just superstitious rubbish. You should be guided by how you feel, not manipulate what you see and pretend it's a message."

"The trouble is I don't know how I feel," Ali said.

"Of course you do. You're just making things difficult for yourself."

"I am not." Ali would have liked to sound indignant, but she couldn't help thinking there might be some truth in Adelaide's guess. She could have made things easier for herself by giving up Noah for adoption, or swallowing her pride and asking her parents to take them in. She couldn't face another argument though over her wasting her time painting, getting involved with the boy they'd warned her about, or how she spoiled Noah by playing with him and reading him stories.

"You could paint here," Adelaide suggested, bringing Ali back to the present.

"In the churchyard?" She didn't think she'd told Adelaide about her painting, but maybe she'd seen her sketching and guessed.

"Why not? It's pretty enough and you'd not be putting anyone to trouble."

"That's true, but I need space to store the wet canvasses."

"Room enough in the guesthouse, I dare say."

She had mentioned where Simon lived and worked, and Adelaide was right; he'd be only too pleased to help out. Although she worried it might be encouraging him unfairly, she decided to ask. Painting again would make her happier, it could bring in more money and it would help her to think. Ali thanked her strange new friend and went to find Simon.

"Of course you can. Actually I was thinking the old summer house might make a good studio for you if we put new glass panels in the roof. I had a look the other day and the old ones still keep the rain out, but they're so covered in mould they keep out the light too."

"I could clean them," Ali suggested. She didn't mind getting up on a ladder, and tidying up the summerhouse would go some way to paying him for the use of it.

A week later, the glass was almost as good as new and Ali's painting was under way. She instinctively knew what would make a good picture. After checking with the vicar, Reverend Gerry Grande, who'd been delighted with the idea, she'd positioned her easel in the older part of the churchyard. She was creating a big landscape, really big, with gravestones and surrounding wildflowers in the foreground and the village beyond. It had taken her a couple of attempts to find the exact spot which would produce the very best result. She discovered one particular stone, ornately shaped at the top with entwined hearts, that made the perfect focal point. Once that was correctly located on her canvas everything else seemed to fall into place.

Ali had also begun lots of studies of wildflowers and other pretty details; much smaller pictures she could sell cheaply to tourists. That would work she knew. They'd be drawn by the big one and buy the smaller ones.

"Will it put you off if I look?" It was Adelaide who asked. "Sorry, I gave you a start."

"I was concentrating. Can you just give me a moment?"

Adelaide seemed to melt away as Ali captured the way the shadow of the church spire leapfrogged over the gravestones and merged with them almost like water or time flowing away from her.

"There, you can look now. I've finished for the day. There's not much to see yet though."

Adelaide studied the painting. "I see what you mean, but I'm sure it will be wonderful, my dear. Now come, I have something to show you."

"A sign?"

"Yes, but you'll have to tell me what it's a sign of." Adelaide pointed out a group of daisies growing in a heart shape close to the attractive stone Ali was using in her painting. "What do they tell you?"

"They could be a sign about the importance of love but they don't tell me if I should marry Simon."

"Look closer. See, it's really two patches. A broken heart might be a sign you shouldn't marry."

"No! No, I don't believe that's what they mean."

"Neither do I. The plants are growing and spreading, soon the clumps will knit together. It could be a sign that together you'll be a whole, he'll mend your broken heart and you'll make his swell with happiness."

That sounded a bit more likely to Ali.

"Or maybe it's not a sign at all?" Adelaide continued. "Perhaps someone just planted them in that shape. They are on a grave."

"That does seem the likeliest explanation." Especially when she considered the shape of the gravestone. Disappointed, Ali packed up her things and said goodbye to Adelaide.

That evening Simon came to tea and Noah asked him, "Are you going to be my Daddy soon?"

The surprise on Simon's face showed Ali he'd not prompted the question, but of course he wouldn't do that. Simon was waiting patiently for her answer. Too patiently? Wouldn't he be more insistent if he really loved her?

"I'd like that very much, Noah," Simon said. "But it's up to Mummy and she needs to think very carefully about whether it's the right thing to do. Important decisions can take a long time."

Noah, who could make choosing which sweets to buy with his pocket money last longer than the time it took him to eat them, nodded his head. "Simon is nice, Mummy," he helpfully pointed out.

"Yes love, he is." And she didn't have a queue of other men to choose from, but that wasn't the issue.

After Simon had read a bedtime story to Noah, Ali explained about her search for a sign.

"I'll look too. I'm so sure we should get married that there must be some way to prove it to you."

Ali wasn't surprised when Adelaide again came to watch her paint. Somehow, no matter how strange she looked and how odd that she seemed to have nothing else to do, it seemed that being in the churchyard, talking to Ali was where she belonged.

"How are you getting on?" Adelaide asked.

"The painting is going well."

"That's not what I meant."

Ali knew that, but didn't have an answer.

"You haven't found your sign because you've not been looking," Adelaide said.

"I have."

"Not for the right thing. You tell yourself you're looking for a sign about whether or not to marry, but really you're searching for one which says you should. Doesn't that show what you really want?"

Was that true? Yes, she realised it was. Some of the things she'd hoped might be the sign she wanted she'd dismissed because they didn't provide the answer she wanted. "You're right, I do want to marry Simon, but that doesn't mean I should."

"Why shouldn't you? He'll provide a home for you and your boy and you'll be able to paint without hindrance. You'll get a good start selling your pictures, build up some money and in a few years your son will change schools. If you split up then you'd get money and be in a much better situation than now. I don't see how you can lose."

"That's just it. I can't, but he might. I thought I was in love with Noah's father and loved in return. It really hurt when we split up, but I see now neither of us truly loved the other. Simon does love me and I don't want to hurt him."

"Because you love him?"

"Yes, yes I do." Of course she did, however could she have doubted it?

"And he loves you. I'd say you stand a better chance of happiness if you marry than if you're apart."

"Oh, Adelaide! You're right of course. You are my sign."

She gathered together her painting equipment and went in search of Simon.

The lady who cleaned at the guest house said, "He's gone out looking for you."

"He'll be back soon then I expect. Will you tell him I'm out in my studio, please?"

The moment Simon returned she told him of her decision.

"That's wonderful, Ali." He pulled her into his arms and kissed her. There was no doubting he was pleased, but he didn't seem surprised.

"Was it calling the summerhouse my studio that gave you a clue?" she asked him.

"That and the fact that I'd found your sign."

"Where?"

"In the churchyard. I was coming to ask you how I'd know the sign if I saw it and I almost walked into it."

"The heart shaped patch of daisies?"

"Oh, was that it? I saw something else. Shall I show you?"

"Yes please."

As they walked to the churchyard, Ali asked, "Did you see my friend Adelaide?"

"Your friend?"

"She often comes to talk to me when I'm painting."

"Oh. No, I didn't see anyone and I'm not sure who she can be. As far as I know there's no one in the village with that name. No one living anyway. Here we are, here's your sign." Simon pointed to the gravestone with the design of entwined hearts. It wasn't easy to read the inscription, but by tracing it with her fingers Ali read, *Here lie Simon Bevitt and his wife Adelaide (Ali) Bevitt. Together in life 67 years. Together in love for eternity.*

"What do you think? That's our sign, isn't it?"

"Yes it is." Close enough at least. Adelaide had been the sign, as she'd said. She'd left her beloved Simon's side for just long enough to ensure another couple could share the same love she was enjoying for eternity.

8. Al The Simple Genie

Colin gave my lamp a very cursory wipe, but I materialised into genie form anyway. I'm nice like that. Plus I love it when my lamp gets polished, so like to reward those who bother.

"Oh! Wow, there really is a genie! I thought that was just a story Mum used to tell me when I was scared of monsters under the bed." Colin said. "What's your name?"

I've been through this introduction thing before. Once it's translated into english my name is long and humans tend to stop paying attention after the first fourteen syllables. Colin is actually Colin Arthur Montgomery Jones, but nobody, even the mother who named him eighteen years ago, ever bothers with all that. Maybe after however many centuries I'd been on this planet, it was time to adapt?

"I'm Al," I told him. Nothing bad happened

"And you'll grant me three wishes?" Colin asked.

Simplifying the truth had worked the first time so I gave it another go. "Yeah, that's right, Colin."

"Excellent," he said.

I immediately decided to de-complicate every aspect of my life.

Colin started that thing humans do of asking me loads and loads of questions. In order to maintain my new simple life, I interrupted. "I'm not sure how I got in here or when or how. All I know is that I can grant you three wishes. If one of those is to send me home then I'm released, although I'm honour bound to point out you're under absolutely no obligation to do that. And," I hurried on, cutting off his next question, "If you don't, I go back into the lamp until the next person comes along for their wishes and I get another chance at freedom."

Colin switched from the asking me questions phase to saying he couldn't believe it part. Then to wondering what to wish for part, then back to not believing it. All totally normal, as was his next move.

"I suppose I can prove it's true with a test. I wish my shirt was blue."

I tried not to look as exasperated as I felt. I get that humans doubt their wishes will be granted but can't fathom why, if they have any hope they'll come true, they waste so many. I've heard them wish a red traffic light would change to green, when they know it'll happen anyway in less time than they took deciding which socks to wear. Or that'll it will stop raining, even though they waste most sunny moments staring at some kind of screen. Or wishing someone would phone, apologise, ask them out or whatever, when they could easily make the first move. Wishes aren't unlimited, people – don't waste them!

"Nothing happened," Colin said.

"Of course it didn't. You have shirts in several colours including blue. Although you're technically an adult your mother keeps them washed and ironed for you, so if you'd wanted to be wearing a blue one today, you wouldn't have put on the white."

"I'd like Lilla to fall in love with me."

That was a much better wish but… "Sorry, I can't make that happen. I can't make people different inside, except sometimes when they want to change. I could make her say she loved you, but that wouldn't mean she did."

"I don't want her to say it if it isn't true."

I was pleased about that. Wishes without truth are worthless.

"Can you do things for me, to make her fall in love?"

"Yes, but be careful. If you're wrong about what would work, you'll be changed but she still won't love you. If you ask me for something, money or fame say, and she's attracted, it will be to what you wished for, not to you."

He thought for a long time. "She really, really wants the local library to stay open and asked me to help. I've been campaigning. If we're successful then she'll be pleased and will like me a bit more. Maybe I could build from that into her loving me."

"That's a pretty good strategy." It was better than that, he'd discovered the formula for granting his wishes himself – work at making them happen.

"Can you keep the library open?"

I asked for the details.

"We've had petitions, held demonstrations, talked to people, used social media and even got a few celebrities involved, we…"

"I can't change the past, Colin."

"Oh. no, I suppose not. There's a public meeting on Friday. At the end the man from the council will say whether it will close or not."

"Would it be enough for me to make him say it won't?" I asked.

"I should think so. There will be lots of people there and the press, and as that's the purpose of the meeting I don't think he could back out of it."

"Consider it done. Next wish?"

"I'd like a job. Something worthwhile that I'd be good at."

That one was tricky. Colin's a nice lad and moderately intelligent, but also shy, unassuming, bordering on dull. I asked for a list of possibilities and he brought me the local paper to look at, as he searched online.

"There you go," I said, drawing a red circle around the job which would suit him best.

"Picking up litter in the park?"

It had a fancy title and there was a bit more to it than that, but basically he was correct. "Trust me," I said.

Although doubtful, Colin applied for that job as well as many others. When he's offered it, and nothing else, he'll accept. He'll be really good at it and, because he isn't lazy like the previous person, he will volunteer for lots of training courses. One will be first aid. During his career, Colin will save three lives, treat nineteen people for minor injuries, and deliver a baby. Other courses will teach him about horticulture and Colin Jones will rise to become head groundsman. OK, he'll be the only groundsman, but unlike other parks where teams of contractors come in to do the work, Colin will have responsibility for everything himself. He'll cut the grass, tend the flowers he's yet to choose and plant, and paint the benches in shades he'll one day select. The park will win many awards.

Colin's unassuming nature will mean he's liked and trusted by people, and pride in the park will ensure he's often there, even when off duty. These combined mean he'll be on hand to prevent one suicide, persuade several run away children to return home, point numerous addicts towards recovery, brighten many lonely people's day and make lots of friends. Towards the end of his long and happy life an assistant will be appointed to assist him, so Colin never retires. But I'm getting sidetracked, back to the Jones's living room and Colin's wishes…

I stayed on the shelf for a couple of days, until Lilla came round after a hard day's campaigning to keep the library open. Colin's mum, Susan, provided a pot of tea and plates of sandwiches and cake before tactfully leaving them alone.

Nervous Colin gulped down three cups of tea and then had to excuse himself. In his absence Lilla picked up my lamp and gently polished it with the sleeve of her sweater. Of course I materialised into genie form.

"Oh!" she said. They always do.

We didn't have long and I was still really liking the simplicity thing, so I said, "Hi, I'm Al. You get one wish, then I'm back into the lamp."

"In that case I wish Colin would fall in love with me."

"OK. On Friday, he'll do just that. Byeee!"

I was back into the lamp and she was back sitting on the sofa, and had decided she must have imagined the whole thing, in plenty of time for Colin's return.

On the Friday evening Colin came in and whispered, "Al, are you there?"

I materialised as my genie self.

"It worked, Al! Well, it's starting to anyway. It was incredible. The council bloke stood up, holding loads of papers, but instead of reading a speech or going through all the petitions and everything, he just said the library would stay open. Everyone was really surprised and happy."

I doubted the council official was happy, but as he'd have been a lot more surprised than everyone else, that evened things out.

"And then Lilla kissed me!"

"There you go then, she's in love."

"Are you sure?"

"Totally positive. Anything else happen today?"

"I got a job offer."

"Congratulations."

"It was the litter picking one."

"Perfect. You'll be good at it and you'll enjoy it and you'll make a difference."

"You sound very sure."

"I'm a genie, Colin. I know this stuff."

"Right. OK then. I think I have one wish left?"

"You do."

"Then I wish to release you. You can go back home."

That was really nice of him and I said so, before dematerialising. What Colin didn't know was that I wasn't actually his genie, so couldn't grant his wishes. Same went for Lilla's. OK, so I helped out as much as I could, but I only had the power to do that because it helped with the wish I was supposed to be granting. Sadly, because I wasn't Colin's genie, he had no power to release me. Instead of going home I just went back into the lamp until his mum was alone in the living room. Then I reappeared in the form she recognised.

"Oh! It's you," Susan said. "Sorry, it's been eighteen years since I saw you and I was a sleep deprived new mother then. If I did take in your name I've forgotten it now."

"I've changed it to Al."

"It suits you. Do you know, I thought I'd imagined you."

"I get that a lot."

"So far my wish has come true," Susan said.

"You remember it then?"

"It's all I've ever wanted – for my little boy to be safe and happy and loved."

"He will be forever, I promise. Now, how about your other two wishes?"

"I've been thinking about those."

"Even though you didn't think I was real?"

"People are allowed fantasies, aren't they?"

I have mine, so I suppose that's only fair. "Come on then, wish number two."

She shook her head. "You know how they say you should be careful what you wish for, in case you get it?"

I didn't, but it's good advice.

"If you'd asked me a few weeks ago I'd have said another cat. I lost Jasper you see."

"That's the one you'd been stroking when I first materialised?" She had been giving my lamp a bit of a clean up, but the cat was getting most of her attention.

"No, that was Brandy. Cats don't live as long as people, you see. After Brandy went I wasn't going to have another, but Colin missed her too, so we got Jasper. I'm glad we did, but I don't think I can take the pain of losing another."

"So what you want is a cat which lives forever?"

"Yes, but such things don't exist, and you told me that you can only grant the possible."

"That's true," I said, because it is.

"So, my wish is that you can have my remaining wishes."

"Oh!" I said, finally sympathetic about the humans' burst of confusion and disbelief when they get offered this opportunity.

"I wish to go home," I said. Nothing happened.

"You're still here," Susan said. "Where is home anyway?"

"I don't know," I admitted.

"So you don't know what it's like?"

"Nope."

"In that case you can't really wish to go back."

"You're right. That's why I'm still here."

"You're welcome to stay if you like, and make this your home."

"That's very kind," I told her. "Did you know genies live forever?"

"No, I didn't," Susan said.

"And that we don't actually live in lamps?"

"No!"

"We just dematerialise from this form and rematerialise as a lamp. It's tradition, but we can pick any shape we like."

Then I dematerialised and rematerialised as a rather handsome grey cat, jumped onto Susan's lap and purred as she stroked me. That was all my wishes come true.

9. Papering Over the Cracks

"Is it ready now, Mum?" Ethan asked.

He was making hallowe'en masks from papier mâché, moulded over a balloon, just as Chrissie had done when she was his age. Some things never changed. He'd been building up the paper layer by impatient layer for several days and was eager to get to the next stage of the process. No doubt, as a child, she'd been just as eager to stop putting in the dull, routine work and get on with more exciting things.

Chrissie tapped the paper covered balloon and smiled. "Yes, it's nice and dry now."

"So I can burst it!"

She made him sit down with a cushion on his lap before giving him her darning needle. "Do it gently."

Ethan braced himself as he stuck the needle into the balloon, which was already a bit soft. Instead of the expected bang it quietly deflated with barely a sigh. That had echoes of Chrissie's life too. Not of her childhood, but of her marriage.

Chrissie took the darning needle from Ethan so he had both hands free to pull the deflated balloon free. Then she offered him the scissors. "Do you want me to start you off?"

"I can do it."

"OK, then. Begin at the bottom where the end of the balloon was sticking out, and go slowly and carefully."

Chrissie recalled all the build up before the wedding and the excitement of the day itself. The honeymoon had been blissful and the first few months of married life very happy. Soon she'd fallen pregnant; much sooner than they'd planned. Sooner than they could really afford. Chrissie didn't have a comfortable pregnancy. Thom didn't ignore that, but working long hours to pay for what the baby would need, meant he wasn't around much. The needs of their young son kept her and Thom busy. Then their daughter came along. It was only recently she'd even had time to worry their relationship had lost its sparkle.

"Oh no, it's gone wrong!" Ethan said. He'd been too impatient and cracked his papier mâché sphere trying to cut it in two. He looked devastated.

"Don't worry love, we can mend it," Chrissie reassured him.

Together they cut eyeholes and papered over the cracks in the two pieces. All they needed was a day or so to dry out and no one would know they'd ever been anything other than perfect.

Papering over the cracks was what she and Thom were doing with their marriage, wasn't it? Putting on a show, pretending everything was OK. He didn't complain about the toys strewn across the floor. She didn't nag about the toy chest lid he'd promised to fix. He said it was nice to have time with the kids when she worked in the evenings. She said it was nice to get a break from them, as she took orders in the restaurant, and carried plates and ignored her aching feet. Chrissie served other couples out on date nights who'd got dressed up and made a real effort for each other. On the rare occasions she and Tom spent the evening together they shared a bath and then a take-away watching a trashy film in their dressing gowns.

A few days later Ethan had two sturdy half circles of papier mâché ready for painting. One, Chrissie guessed, was to be a scary monster for him. The other was for his sister and would probably be painted in brightest pink.

Holes were needed to thread through the elastic which would hold the masks on their faces. She provided him with a metal skewer with which to do the job.

"I don't want to, Mum. I might break them again," Ethan said.

"They won't be any use if you don't, love. I'll help you."

She held a cork against the outside of the masks as Ethan carefully pushed through the skewer. This time he followed Chrissie's advice to work carefully and slowly, which resulted in four nice neat holes right where he needed them. He used the darning needle again to get the elastic to go through, then tied nice big knots so it stayed in place.

"Well done, love!"

Proudly Ethan gave one mask to his sister. They set about decorating them with absorbed concentration.

Chrissie had been slightly wrong in her assumptions. There was no scary monster for Ethan, but a happy smiling face. One with vampire fangs admittedly, but then it was hallowe'en. His sister's fairy princess was a far paler shade of pink than anticipated, on account of being a ghost.

"She got ghosted saving the handsome Prince, Mummy. She likes being a ghost because she gets lots of marshmallow."

Chrissie smiled at her daughter's imagination despite not totally following her logic. She was suitably impressed by the excellent work both children had made of their masks.

Had she and Tom done such a good job papering over any cracks in their marriage? It wasn't perfect and sometimes they forgot to bite their tongues and said hurtful things, but not often and they always kissed and made up. The only real problem was that the long hours they worked between them meant they barely spent any time together as a couple. That night would be different. Chrissie didn't have to work and Thom's parents were taking the children trick or treating and keeping them for the night.

"Are you two going to do something fun?" her mother-in-law asked after she'd admired the children's masks and costumes.

"Oh yes, we've got a great evening planned."

Chrissie ran the bath whilst Thom fixed the toy chest lid. After a soak together they snuggled up on the sofa eating pizza, drinking a bottle of cheap fizz, and watching a silly horror film. It was bliss. Moments like that weren't papering over the cracks of their marriage but the glue which held the couple together.

10. It'll Be The Death Of Me

"This wretched car will be the death of me," I muttered after banging my head on the boot while putting in my suitcase. More than once, as I was about to set off on a drive, I'd had the feeling something would go wrong – and I was quite often right.

Knowing that, I was leaving for the airport early, and had my friendly neighbour and his jump leads on standby in case it refused to start.

"I did say you were worrying for nothing," he said as the car burst into life.

It seemed he was right. The fuel levels hadn't mysteriously dropped and no warning lights flashed on the dashboard. The engine ran smoothly as I drove away and I had no trouble keeping up with the other traffic when I joined the motorway. If things continued like that, I'd be early. When my friends eventually arrived I'd tell them about my silly fear the car would somehow prevent me joining them for a week's fun in the sun and we'd laugh about it.

"What the…" The rest of my terrified scream was cut off by a faceful of airbag, although in my dazed state it took me a little while to understand that. Even longer to realise that my windscreen was shattered. I don't know how I got through the traffic, but I'd reached the hard shoulder.

Once my predicament dawned on me, I crawled across to the passenger side of the car, grabbed my bag, let myself out and stepped over the barrier to safety. I'd hit that at an angle, denting it and wrecking the lights on the lefthand side. The impact must have been what set off the airbag. Although still feeling shaky I managed to call the breakdown service.

"I'm a woman on my own," I told them, hoping it was true that fact made me a bit more of a priority.

"Someone will be with you as soon as possible. Should be under an hour."

Then I phoned my mate Lindsay to tell her what was going on. After she'd checked I was OK she pointed out our holiday was insured.

"Call the company, Mira. Maybe they can sort you out with a taxi or something?"

As I was on hold to them, and trying to get airbag dust out my eyes, hair and clothes, several emergency vehicles screamed by. I was reminded of Aunt Hilda. If she'd known what was happening, instead of offering sympathy for my near miss and shock she'd have said, "See, there's always folk worse off."

Aunt Hilda wasn't a real relation. She was the midwife who delivered me. There had been a storm which brought down trees making the road to my parents' home impassable, so Hilda had walked three miles in torrential rain. Mum reckoned she'd saved my life and had asked her to be my godmother. I don't know why Hilda accepted, or did the job she did, as she didn't seem to like children much. Even so, she insisted on me going to stay with her for a week every summer holiday. The location, in rural Devon was wonderful – when she let me enjoy it.

My memories were interrupted by the arrival of the breakdown truck. The driver, Roisin, was a surprise. She can't have weighed more than seven stone, and part of that was made up of a long plait of gorgeous red hair. She was very efficient. It seemed to take her only minutes to set up warning signs, remove my luggage from the boot, get her truck into position and winch on my awful car.

"Don't look so worried," Roisin said as I joined her in the cab. "The damage is mostly superficial. It'll be fixed up and back on the road in no time."

"That's what I'm worried about."

"Sorry?"

Roisin's sympathy made me glad I'd decided against telling her I'd hoped it would be a write off as, ever since my godmother gave me the car, I'd disliked it and soon came to think it was cursed or something. That does sound a bit mad unless you know the history. As Hilda hadn't liked me much I'd felt the gift was a sort of trap. I'd hoped to get something a bit sporty and fun. That would have needed financial help from my parents and they weren't prepared to give it when Aunt Hilda had provided me with a dreary old heap, which was relatively cheap to insure.

After Hilda died I had all kinds of trouble with the car. It actually broke up my engagement, by stopping me meet my fiancé on numerous occasions and making him think I was deliberately messing him about. Twice it just wouldn't start, but when he came round later it worked perfectly. It ran out of petrol even though I'd checked the gauge the day before and seen there was plenty. Three times I had a puncture when I was on the way to see him. The last time meant I hadn't made it in time to sort out our finances, life insurance, and all that kind of thing just prior to the wedding. It had been the final straw and he dumped me. I'd tried to sell the car, so I could get another, but every time anyone came to look it either wouldn't go, or made strange noises when it did.

"Will you still be able to make your flight if we do that?" Roisin asked.

"Sorry, I wasn't paying attention," I admitted. She'd been using her cab radio and chatting, but I'd zoned out.

"It'll be the shock. There's some food in the glove box. That might help a bit, but it's only healthy stuff. My partner is a tyrant that way!"

As I rummaged through the nutrition bars and packs of dried fruit I remembered Aunt Hilda refusing to allow me to drink Coke and limiting sweets to just after meals. I'd thought it was mean, but of course she'd been concerned about my teeth. Her other rules, such as not allowing me to walk the cliff path alone, were no doubt intended to keep me safe rather than spoil my fun.

"You said I might still make my flight?"

"I was going to tow your car back to the garage and then we'd arrange transport home or wherever you needed to go, but I could drive straight to the airport now."

"Please try that."

"Great. The crash will slow us up a bit, as I'll have to take a less direct route and other traffic has been diverted that way, but hopefully you'll make it."

"Crash?" That didn't make sense as Roisin wouldn't be there if I hadn't crashed. Then I noticed we'd left the motorway and remembered the ambulances.

"Awful. Six dead and more with serious injuries. Seems weird to say but your windscreen shattering was a stroke of luck in a way. If you'd carried on you'd have got caught up in it. Those close to it will be there hours as they've got to cut people out."

I couldn't help wondering exactly how close I'd have been if the car hadn't once again developed a problem. There wasn't much time to think about that, as Roisin had got the breakdown truck as close to the airport entrance as she could, and I made a run for it. Thanks to her help, and calls from the travel insurers, I was whizzed through check-in and met up with my friends in the departures lounge.

After hugs and exclamations of relief, Lindsay asked if I'd seen the news.

"That terrible crash? I almost saw it happen."

"Actually I meant this." She handed me a newspaper, folded to show a photo of my ex fiancé and the headline – 'Is this multiple widower a serial killer?'

I opened the page to read the article. Unbeknown to me he'd been married twice before we met. His first wife had died suddenly and unexpectedly. He'd inherited everything, plus benefitted from a large life insurance payout. The exact same thing had happened with his second wife. He'd married again after we split up and his third wife was currently fighting for her life in hospital after what he claimed had been an accident.

"That could have been you," Lindsay whispered.

"No chance, not with Aunt Hilda and my trusty little car looking after me." I didn't know for sure how many times between them they'd saved my life, but at last I was grateful.

11. In Their Shoes

Christmas isn't a time of consumerism and greed, not in our family. We show compassion to those less fortunate than ourselves. Remember that, but for some lucky twist of fate, strange coincidence, the grace of God, we'd be in their shoes.

I don't know when it first began. The tradition. The competition. I've been here nine years and it's always been spoken of as though it's a thing which always was.

We begin on Christmas Eve. Each of us go out, looking for homeless people, who resemble ourselves as closely as possible. Physically I mean – you can't judge a person's character when they're sheltering from hunger and cold in a discarded cardboard box. We go in pairs or groups, to help get a good match in terms of sex, age, height, skin tone and face shape, and to ensure there's no cheating.

Once we all have a guest we take them home and feed them. They each get to take a shower, have a shave if they wish, and are offered a haircut. None of us is professional in that respect, but Cousin Ellen can manage a quick tidy up. Our guest is given a set of our clothes and invited to sleep in our bed for the night. The family all sleep in the lounge. It's comfortable enough, especially when we think how others will spend the night before Christmas.

In the morning, our guests receive breakfast and a small gift. Something practical – socks, toiletries, stuff like that. We play games and sing festive songs until it's time for lunch. After that is when the points are scored. Though they don't know the rules until after, the winner is whichever guest eats the most candy canes by midnight.

Today it's Michael's guest.

He, Michael, goes up to what was once his bedroom, puts on his guest's discarded rags and returns with his own identification documents and bank cards. He hands them to his guest. "You're me now," he says. To the other guests he says, "Christmas is over," and he and they return to the cold dark streets.

"Welcome to the family, Michael," we say to the new member of the family.

12. A Charmed Life

I barely looked at the mug, but that was enough to send it falling out the cupboard on to my kitchen floor. I'm not usually clumsy but sometimes, when I'm upset, accidents happen.

"It didn't smash!" Vicki 's shocked reaction suggested that was further reason for her to to be angry with me.

Usually I'd have joked about how lucky I was, but she was in no mood to hear about my good fortune. "Of course it didn't, I've got cushioned flooring," I said.

"No you haven't!" She reached down. "Oh! I could have sworn they were real tiles."

"Perhaps that's not the only thing you've been mistaken about?" I asked.

"It isn't," she snapped. "I thought we were friends."

"We are," I said, hoping it was still true.

"Then why charm yourself into the job I wanted?"

"You wanted the promotion?" I probably sounded as surprised as Vicki had about the mug. I knew a few others had applied for the job, but thought the main reason they'd done that was to prevent it going to someone from outside. That's caused problems in the past.

"Why wouldn't I?" Vicki demanded.

Because she wanted to have babies and be a stay at home mum. She hadn't actually said that, but I'd been so sure it was what she really wanted… Oh dear, what had I done?

Everyone else had congratulated me on the promotion, saying I'd be perfect for the role, but not Vicki. Her look had said she'd like to burn me at the stake. Later she'd barged past me hissing, "I'm on to you."

The words had made me shiver. Although she couldn't know for sure, it was possible she'd guessed the truth. Because of that, and because I didn't want her to stay angry with me, I'd used my persuasive powers to get her to come to my place after work and talk about it.

She'd followed me home, accepted my offer of tea and sat on one of my kitchen chairs, just as she'd done many times before. Everything was going fine until I dropped the mug and broke the spell.

"You lead a charmed life, Tina."

She's said things like that before and I've managed to laugh it off. Not this time.

"You always have all the luck," Vicki continued. "And if it doesn't came naturally you fix things so you get what you want. I know what tricks you played to get promoted."

"Tricks?" That's not the word I'd have used.

"It's pretty obvious how you got round Mr Roberts. He's always looking down our tops."

She thought I'd slept my way to promotion? Thinking it might be better if she believed that, I just shrugged.

"Maybe you got away with it this time, but you better watch out – what goes around comes around."

She was right about that. I could have pointed out that insulting the person who was just about to become her new line manager wasn't a good idea, but I didn't. There's no way I'd use my power to hurt her, I'd much rather patch up our friendship.

"I'm sorry you're upset over this," I said. "I honestly didn't think you were bothered about the promotion."

Vicki looked into my eyes for a moment. "If you say so." She didn't sound totally convinced, but I felt she wanted to believe me.

Conjuring up positive vibes, I made her tea in the mug I'd dropped. "Perhaps it's the mug which is lucky, not me?" I jokingly suggested.

"Could be." She gave a brief smile. "Having to get jiggy with lecher Roberts isn't exactly lucky."

"No." I shuddered. That man was going to be my immediate supervisor and he was truly awful, but I really couldn't do to him what he deserved.

Vicki's face wobbled and I hoped she was going to laugh over the idea of me seducing the horrid Mr Roberts, but instead she started crying.

"Come on, tell me what's up. It's not about the job, is it?" I coaxed.

Between sobs, she told me I was right about her not wanting promotion; and why. "All I want is a baby." I learned her doctor had said, although it wasn't entirely impossible, the odds were against her. "I did apply for the job, but only because I thought having a career might somehow make not having a family less painful. It wouldn't have helped and you'll make a much better manager than me."

Incredibly relieved that what I'd done hadn't been an awful mistake, I hugged her tight.

She hugged me back. "Sorry, Tina. Of course you wouldn't have done what I said… with Mr Roberts. I don't know what came over me."

I did. "Hormones?" I suggested. "Some women do get emotional at, you know, that time of month."

She stared at me. "But it isn't… well, it is, but I'm not... Oh my god! Do you think …?"

Vicki rushed off to get a pregnancy test, leaving me very, very relieved. And absolutely determined never ever to interfere in anyone's life ever again.

As soon as she'd gone I reversed the spell on my kitchen tiles. I never did like that cushioned stuff, but at the time it was all I could think of to explain about the mug. Some people say tiles are cold but that doesn't worry me. The myth about witches' feet not touching the floor is true. So is the one about all our deeds coming back to us threefold.

Suddenly I had a brilliant thought. I was due some good karma for the pregnancy spell I'd done for Vicki. That would cancel out giving Mr Roberts exactly what he deserved. He'd make an excellent toad and after he'd hopped off I'd be in line for his job. It was tempting, very tempting.

13. What I've Become

It's hard to tell the difference sometimes. Between creativity and destruction, I mean. That guy who created the atom bomb for example. Clever science, and he probably meant well, but afterwards he considered himself the destroyer of worlds. Rightly perhaps; his discovery has killed I don't know how many thousands, brought misery, fear and suffering to many more. I'm not in his league, but I am desperate. Maybe only another writer could understand. Or an editor, publisher, competition judge. You know what it's like for us, don't you?

I haven't destroyed anything, except maybe the corners of my mind. I think I've created new worlds. Not think. I know. I've built wonderful settings, crafted intricate plots, developed intriguing characters. But if the magazines don't print my stories all I've done is destroy pristine white pages, killed trees. Not that I care that much about trees, but you get my point.

My competition entries; if they're not shortlisted, at least, then what's the point? And my novels. They're out there for you to download, but if you don't do it I've just murdered pixels in the womb. See? Destructive. Destruction from creativity, just like him; Oppenheimer.

So I've diversified. I've created a virus. Not physical or virtual: both. If you touched my manuscript or opened my email then you're contaminated by my plague. There's an antidote of course; I'm not entirely irresponsible. Not completely without mercy. Send me a contract, proof copy, prize or receipt as appropriate. I will supply your cure. If you're quick enough. If it's not too late. Otherwise you'll be getting one of those 'thank you for the opportunity... Careful consideration... Regret to inform... Good luck elsewhere' letters. Not that you'll read it. Not that you'll read, or reject, or accept, ever again.

You're reluctant to believe me I know. But your computer is already running more slowly. It's not backing up. You feel sleepy and know no dreams will come. Read and publish my stories. Do it now while you can still see the words.

Do

    it

   n

    o

      w

    .

14. Iceberg

Joey's hand reached out. He watched as it trembled, struggling to grasp the brown paper bag. He was afraid, horribly afraid, but he must wrap the bad ice cube before it grew into an iceberg and sank, dragging him down with it. Could it do that? Joey couldn't remember.

He knew he needed medication, but the medicine bottle was empty. Mary would bring more; if he could only stay calm until she came. Joey took a deep breath, thrust a hand into his mother's oven mitt, moved as close to the fallen ice cube as he dared and grabbed. With his arm outstretched, he dropped the cube into the bag. Using the gloved hand, he wrapped the paper over and over until the square piece of ice was transformed into a damp ball of paper. Joey breathed out. He wrapped elastic bands around the parcel and threw it into the kitchen pedal bin. Would that be enough to hold it?

He picked up the newspaper and sat with it, on the bin. He tried to read. He mustn't let Mary know he was afraid. He took his lucky pen from his pocket. He'd started the crossword by the time Mary came home.

"I've got your medication. Would you like some now?" she asked. "It's OK, don't get up, I'll bring it over."

She poured chilli sauce onto a plastic measuring spoon and handed it to him. As he swallowed and coughed, she filled a tumbler with water.

"Ice?"

Joey began to cry.

"Drink it as it is then, Joey. Drink the water and you'll feel better."

He sipped and sobbed alternately. As he drank the last few drops, he was once again almost under control.

"Did you have to put something in the bin?" Mary asked.

Joey nodded. He didn't look at his sister.

"That's OK Joey. If you don't want something, then you should put it in the bin."

"Really?"

"Really."

"It was an ice cube, Mary. Should you put ice cubes in the bin? Do other people do that? Do you?"

"Perhaps, if there was something wrong with it."

He looked at her now. "There was, Mary. There was something wrong. It was bigger than the others."

"Maybe the tray was filled unevenly?"

"I hadn't thought of that." He dropped his gaze, and began to fidget.

"What did you think of?"

"I don't know."

"Yes you do, Joey."

"I can't remember."

"Joey, look at me."

He glanced up. She smiled and he tried to do the same.

"Joey, I'm your big sister. I remember when you jumped of the roof with an umbrella, thinking it would be your parachute. I remember when you tried to paint the dog orange, because Mum said he wasn't very bright. I was there when you started that fire, the one that scared you.

I've seen you do lots of daft things, and helped you clear up after them. Joey, trust me now."

"I feel silly."

"Tell me."

"I thought it was bad. That it was growing, that it would get bigger and bigger. I felt all cold and wet where it touched me. I thought there was bad stuff in it. I was scared, Mary."

"You're not scared now are you?"

"No."

"What did you do with it?"

"I put it in a paper bag, so I couldn't see it."

"That explains the tomatoes on the floor."

"Sorry, Mary. I had to do it quick. I thought it was still growing. It felt bigger when I'd wrapped it. I put lots of elastic bands on it and put it in the bin. Then I sat on it, so it couldn't grow anymore."

"That was clever."

"Was it?"

"Yes, Joey. You got really frightened, but you remembered what you've been told. You didn't keep looking at what made you scared. You know when you're scared you should go somewhere safe, or get somebody to take away the scary thing. You remembered that."

"You weren't here, Mary. I took my medicine, lots of it, but it didn't help."

"I'm sorry I wasn't here, Joey, but you did really well without me. You did everything right."

"I'm glad you're back now."

He reached to hug her, but she'd taken a step back.

"Joey, shall we look in the bin?"

"Can't you just take it away?"

"No, Joey. Now you get up and stand over there by the door. I'll look."

Mary took the soggy bag from the bin. Joey didn't watch her, he didn't like looking at her burnt arms. They reminded him of the fire. He didn't want to think about the fire. Mary placed the sodden paper on the kitchen table and removed the tightly wound elastic bands. There was nothing inside.

"Where's it gone?" Joey asked.

"It's melted."

"Just an ordinary ice cube then?"

"Yes, Joey."

"I was frightened of an ordinary ice cube." Joey cried.

"You were scared Joey, but you were brave too. You didn't know it was ordinary when you wrapped it up."

"Brave?"

"Yes, Joey. I think you're getting better."

"Yes, I am."

"I think we should go back and see Doctor McKenzie. You could tell him how much better you're getting."

"I don't know. He asks funny questions. He wanted to take me away from you."

"I won't let him do that. But, Joey, will you see him again?"

"I don't know."

"Please, Joey."

"I will then, if you'll come with me?"

"I'll always be with you, Joey," she whispered, her words almost drowned by a shout from another room.

"Joey, who are you talking to?"

"No one."

His mother came into the kitchen. She glanced round at the spilt tomatoes, soggy paper, elastic bands and chilli sauce bottles.

"Are you all right, Joey?"

"I was thinking about Mary."

"Oh, Joey," his mum hugged him. "You miss her, we all do. I wish I knew how to help you."

"I'll go back to Doctor McKenzie, if you want."

"Thank you, Joey."

15. Thalia Gets Lucky

On her way to a job interview, Thalia visited a charity shop. She wanted a book to read on the bus journey. Without something to distract her, she knew she'd get nervous.

There was a flimsy green waterproof coat on the floor in front of the bookshelf. Thalia picked it up, intending to return it to the rail, but the latest book by one of her favourite authors was already providing a distraction. A hardback for half what the paperback version would cost. My lucky day, she thought.

"Oh, I'm so glad someone has bought that already!" the assistant exclaimed.

"I'm amazed it's already in here. The paperback hasn't even been released yet."

"I meant that coat thing, dear. The person who donated it said it was lucky and she'd had some wonderful news the day after getting it. She didn't say what, but a baby on the way is my guess."

Thalia, who hadn't realised she was still holding the waterproof, held it up. "I didn't notice it's a maternity one."

"Oh, it isn't. It's one of those one size fits all affairs that you can easily put on over anything. Quite a bargain for 50p, even if it isn't really lucky."

"You're right." It seemed rather mean to say she didn't want it, especially as she'd got such a good deal on the book.

"I think it's right about the luck too. The till had been playing up for weeks, but it's been fine since that arrived. We've been busier than usual too."

Thalia read for a while on the bus, but put the book away a few stops from her destination. She didn't want to get so distracted she missed her stop. She returned the book to her bag and took out the waterproof for a proper look. It was a nice shade of mossy green and had a hood. Inside was a huge label. Rather than a brand name or care instructions, it bore a rhyme.

You'll have good luck if I'm yours for a week.

Keep me longer your future will be bleak.

Put me on loan and you must atone.

Give me away and your luck will stay.

Throw me away and you'll rue the day.

It wasn't great poetry, but it was beautifully embroidered.

A little more luck won't hurt, Thalia thought and pulled the waterproof over her head. As promised it went on easily. She didn't have time to see if it was as easily removed because the bus had reached her stop. Thalia stepped off just as a window cleaner's hose burst. Without the waterproof covering her clothes and hair she would have got drenched and she'd have arrived at the interview looking like a drowned rat.

She shook off as much water as she could, peeled off the waterproof and folded it over her arm so it could dry before going back into her bag. It took Thalia longer than expected to find the office where her interview was to take place, but she was on time when she introduced herself at reception.

"Nice to meet you, Thalia," said a friendly looking man. "I'm Owen. If you'd like to come with me…?" His smile made her even more keen to get the job.

As they rode up in the lift, Owen remarked on her having a wet coat on a dry day. Thalia explained about getting sprayed.

"Lucky for you that you had the coat then."

"Yes, very. Even so, I probably should have left it in reception."

"Leave it here. I'll pick it up when I go back down and look after it for you."

"That's very kind."

"Not at all. Actually I, er…" He blushed. "Ah! We're here!"

As Owen introduced her to the boss, he said, "I think she'll fit in well. She's the sort of person who is ready for anything!"

The interview went well. The boss said the usual, "Thanks for coming, we'll let you know," but not in the usual tone. She became even more optimistic when he gave her a copy of the employment contract to look over while she awaited his decision.

When Thalia returned to reception she told Owen, "I'm hopeful we'll be working together."

"If that's a contract, then we will," Owen said. "He doesn't give them out unless he expects to get them back signed."

"Great! Well, I suppose I'd better collect my coat and go – not that I expect to need it again anytime soon. I think the good weather is expected to last."

"In that case... I was wondering... If it's not too cheeky..."

"What is it, Owen?" She'd already guessed that although friendly he was a little shy, and had been considering saying something more personal in the lift. She was more than happy to provide another opportunity.

"I was wondering if you'd loan me the coat? My nephew is in a school play as a pixie in a couple of days and there's been a problem with his costume. The coat would fit the bill perfectly."

"Oh!" Thalia remembered the rhyme. "No, I won't lend it to you, but I'll give it to you on two conditions. No, three."

"And they are?" Owen asked.

"You give it to your nephew before the play, and make sure he gives it away afterwards."

"Alright, but why?"

Thalia showed Owen the embroidered rhyme. "I have had some luck since I picked it up, so who knows, there could be something in it."

"Perhaps. You said there were three conditions?"

"I want to know what you started to say in the lift, when I said it was kind of you to look after the coat for me. You weren't thinking of your nephew then, were you?"

He blushed again. "Not entirely, no. I was thinking it gave me an excuse to speak to you again. The coat, it's mine now?"

"It is, yes."

"Then let's test how lucky it is for me. Will you come to dinner with me tonight?"

"I'd love to."

"That proves it. It works!"

On the bus home, Thalia decided Owen was right. Whether it really had special powers, or the luck just came from the positive outlook which owning it encouraged, Thalia couldn't say, but she had a strong feeling that both she and Owen would be lucky in love.

16. Restless Nights

Elise couldn't sleep. She didn't think she was particularly anxious about the birth, just physically uncomfortable due to her size.

Terry seemed unsettled too, excited even. He was obviously dreaming. She felt him move in the bed next to her and heard his heavy breathing. Elise reached out and felt his heart pounding.

"Rose, no… I can't, Rose," he moaned.

A man can't help what he says in his sleep, but… One of their colleagues was called Rosemary. Elise should be glad he was saying no. But why had he got into that situation? It wasn't because he sent the wrong signals. Terry didn't send out any. Maybe a man-eater would take that as encouragement enough. Was Rosemary that type? She was covering Elise's maternity leave. Maybe it wasn't just Elise's job she wanted?

It wouldn't be fair to say Terry was secretive exactly, but she'd often found it hard to know what he was thinking and feeling. They'd worked and socialised together for months before she had the teeniest inkling he was attracted to her. In fact if he hadn't got so tongue tied when he suggested they see a film together she wouldn't have realised he didn't mean simply as a friend. Elise would have encouraged him more if she'd known how he felt, but he'd kept his emotional distance so much she'd been afraid to scare him off.

She wasn't surprised when he proposed: she was shocked. Terry didn't take emotional commitment lightly. Elise guessed that was partly because he'd been brought up in a series of foster homes. He said they'd mostly been really kind, but it was clear he would rather have been adopted.

He'd increasingly opened up to her after their engagement. They'd talked about having children and agreed before they married it was something they both wanted. They discussed it again almost two years ago and decided the time was right to try. He'd not shown a great deal of emotion then but when she said she was pregnant he'd been delighted. Was he having second thoughts?

The dream, complete with anguished pleas to Rose, recurred.

Over breakfast she said, "You were talking in your sleep last night."

"Sorry. Hope I didn't wake you?" He seemed genuinely concerned, but he would if he thought he'd let slip an affair, wouldn't he?

"No, I don't think so. I've not been sleeping too well."

He put his hand on her huge belly. "You have nothing to worry about. Everything is looking good and you've followed all the advice. You'll be an absolutely brilliant mum."

Nothing about him being there for her, she noted. He'd reverted to treating her almost as he had before the wedding too. With some men that might be a good thing, but with Terry it left her feeling excluded. Something was definitely wrong.

Elise started looking for clues. It was stupid of course. People in the office often switched chairs so it was no surprise he occasionally had a stray hair on him. There was nothing odd about having colleague's numbers in his phone.

She did too. Dreams were a jumble of things. Calling a woman's name didn't mean anything. At least, it might not.

"Terry, you've been calling the name Rose in your sleep," she said one evening.

"Oh. Would you like a cup of tea?"

"No. I want you to sit down and tell me everything."

"I can't… I know it was wrong, but I couldn't help it."

She tried to contain her distress; it couldn't be good for the baby. "I'm your wife, Terry. I'm pregnant with your child. You can, and will, tell me about this."

He sat quietly, his head bowed. It seemed a long time until he raised his tear streaked face and looked at her. "I thought Rose liked me. When I felt alone, he seemed to be a friend."

"He?"

"Tom Rose. He bullied a lot of the other kids. I was made part of the gang. He made me steal things for him. Shoplifting sweets mostly, but sometimes things from my foster homes, or taking money from smaller kids."

Elise tried to comfort him as he confessed to cheating and lying to the people he'd since realised were the ones who were really on his side.

"You can see now why I was never adopted."

"Not really. They should have seen through that, stopped the bullying…"

"It doesn't matter now. It's in the past and although I've been remembering it, that's not really the problem."

"What is?"

"I've learned to hide my feelings so much. I'm a rubbish husband. What kind of dad will I be?"

"You're a brilliant husband! Why else would I be scared of losing you?"

"How could you think that?"

"Stupid I know. Blame my hormones, but I thought you could be having an affair."

Terry shook his head, looking puzzled. "Yep, that is a stupid thing to think." He pulled her close. "I love you so much, Elise."

She didn't doubt it. "I know, and I love you too."

"But I kept my worries from you and that hurt you. I won't be able to show our child how I feel."

"I'm sure you'll learn." At least that's what she tried to say, as her first contraction gripped. She tried to reassure him as they rushed around making sure everything was ready and contacting the midwife, after her waters broke, and during the drive to hospital.

A few hours later Terry was sobbing and holding his son. "Our boy. Our precious boy. He's beautiful. I love you, son. I'm your daddy and I'm going to look after you." Terry continued in that vein for several minutes, then kissed the boy's head and returned him carefully to Elise so he could feed. "I think it might be OK. I thought it would be difficult to really care, but I already love him."

Elise laughed. "Things will be fine once you learn to show him that, don't you think?"

"Will I be able to?"

"Yes, Terry. You will."

17. Life Saver

Marianne helped her daughter tidy the lounge.

"Those women saved my life," Lynne said as she collected books and a necklace from the lounge floor. "Here, Mum, you'd better put this back on before Denise wakes up and starts playing with it again."

"Thanks, love." Marianne fastened the necklace.

"That's better. I can't remember ever seeing you without it. It looks wrong somehow."

"It feels wrong. One day I'll want to show it to someone and…" What had Lynne said? "Saved your life did you say? Which women and how?" Marianne asked.

"The women who wrote the Pretty Purple Pixie books. When Denise was a toddler and had all that trouble with her teeth, I was desperate for some peace and really felt I was cracking up. Then I got one of those books from the library for her. I almost threw it at her, I expect."

Marianne doubted that. "I don't suppose you did, love. I expect you sat down and read it nicely to her."

"Maybe, but I did want to throw things. I was so tired I couldn't think straight and felt like I was heading for some kind of emotional crisis. Anyway, as soon as Denise spotted the pictures she shut up. I don't suppose she was quiet for long – what toddler is? But those few moments reminded me things would get better. We read every book together. They helped calm me down too. They're lovely, and the illustrations… You can't help smiling when you see them."

Marianne flicked through one of the books, then turned to the front and read the author's and illustrator's names. "That's a coincidence. The lady who drew the pictures is called Celeste and when I was a child, I had a friend called Celeste who was going to save your life."

"What was she, a time traveller? I wasn't around to be saved when you were a child."

"Funny you should mention time travel..." Marianne thought back to Celeste and all the plans they'd had. "Celeste was an inventor. I came up with all kinds of things for her to invent. One was a miracle cure, for... I can't remember what, but I'm afraid I'd imagined my future child suffering from it."

Lynne rolled her eyes and put a hand to her forehead. "Gee, thanks, Mum."

"It wouldn't have been painful, love," Marianne said and grinned. "More beautifully tragic and anyway, I knew Celeste would invent a cure."

"She wanted to be a doctor or scientist?"

"No. I wanted her to be a genius inventor. I'm not sure I gave a thought to what she wanted. A time machine was what I most wanted her to invent. The other things were a warm up for that. Although Celeste was much cleverer than me, I did realise time travel was asking a lot."

"Where, or rather when, did you want to travel too?"

"Now, I suppose. You see, at thirteen I was madly in love with her brother Devon. Celeste knew the daughter of a bank manager wouldn't be allowed to marry the son of an immigrant cleaner from the Caribbean."

"Granny and Grandad aren't racist..."

"No, love, but this was more than fifty years ago. Your grandparents accepted Celeste as my friend and spoke politely to her parents, but things were different then. Celeste believed things would change in the future. She and her brother and others of their generation would get good jobs, become doctors, teachers and bankers and be respected as equals."

"And she was right. All except the bit about bankers being respected." Lynne winked at her mother.

"She was, but I couldn't wait. I wanted her to build us a time machine and take us to the future so I could marry her brother. She did try, I might still have the sketches… It didn't matter though as there was something I hadn't taken into account."

"The laws of Physics?"

"No. Devon."

"What happened to him?"

"Nothing. It's just that he was seventeen and had a life of his own. He had no intention of going along with my plan and falling in love with his kid sister's little pal."

"No taste, some men."

"Exactly. I fell in love with Elvis Presley the week after and he wasn't interested in me either. Celeste kept inventing things though. I'd think of something we needed, such as a device to instantly do our nails, and she invented it."

"She built these things?"

"No, she drew it and I'd decide what extra features it should have and she'd add them on."

"It sounds to me as though you were the inventor if you had all the ideas."

"Maybe, but the ideas didn't come to life until she drew them. My ideas weren't good, but her pictures were."

"Your friend wasn't this Celeste Martin was she? It sounds to me like her childhood with you would have been the perfect apprenticeship for a children's book illustrator."

"That wasn't her surname then, but she probably got married. I suppose it could be her. Is there a picture of the author?"

They looked, but the flyleaf didn't give any further clues to Celeste's identity.

"Did you say you still had some of her drawings?"

"If I have, I know exactly where they'll be. There's a big blue box in the loft."

"Can I go and look? Denise should sleep for at least another half hour."

"You can, although I'll be surprised if you don't wake Denise getting that ladder down."

Lynne went up to the loft and soon returned with a folder of drawings but no Denise. Together, Lynne and Marianne looked through the drawings. One was of a money making machine operated by pixies rather like the ones in Denise's book.

"Mum, these are really good. I'm no expert, but it seems likely that your friend is the same woman who draws the Pretty Purple Pixie books. She wasn't just good for a kid, she had real talent."

"I always thought so. I planned that we'd both make millions from her inventions and have tea together at The Ritz in London, and compare our diamonds, when we were old ladies."

"The Ritz?"

"Yes, it always seemed the height of luxury. Oh well, it wasn't to be. I haven't seen Celeste since we were teenagers. My family moved away and we just lost touch. I didn't forget her though and as a kind of tribute to her, when I started working, I saved each week and eventually bought myself a small diamond." Marianne lifted the pendent on her necklace. "If I ever meet her again, I want to be sure that she sees this."

A couple of weeks later Marianne had a call from Lynne.

"Remember you were talking about tea at the Ritz? How do you fancy doing that tomorrow tomorrow?"

"Bless you, what a lovely thought."

When Lynne arrived she didn't look at all dressed up.

"Don't worry, Mum. It's you who is going to The Ritz, not me."

What a disappointment. It wouldn't be nearly so much fun on her own.

"Hey, don't look like that! I'm not sending you in there on your own," she said as though reading her mother's mind.

"But…"

"I wrote to the publishers of the pixie books and asked if they could pass on a message to Celeste Martin. I asked her to contact me if she really was your old friend. She rang yesterday."

"Oh, Lynne! You are clever."

"Yes, I am. I'm sorry I don't have time to collect you today, but Celeste promised to make sure you get home safely," Lynne explained as she parked the car. "I'll come round tomorrow and hear all about it and you can tell me again how clever I am."

"I'd like that."

Marianne walked into the lobby and looked around.

"Marianne, is that really you?" asked a woman who had to be Celeste.

The two women hugged.

"I'm so pleased to have found you, or at least to have been found by you."

"By my daughter actually. Right after telling me how you saved her life."

"I was supposed to do that, wasn't I? Looking at you and knowing how I feel, I almost believe the time machine must have worked too. We can't really be over sixty, can we?"

"No, I just don't think that's possible. So how about your other inventions? Did you make the thing to apply make-up in seconds?" Marianne asked.

"No, although these days that certainly would be useful. In a way I did manage the pixie money making machine."

"Yes, I know how successful your books are."

A waiter approached.

"We need a really big pot of tea, please; we have a lot to talk about," Celeste informed him.

When he'd taken their order and left, Celeste leant across the table.

"That pendant you're wearing, is that a real diamond?"

"Of course! Now, show me yours."

Celeste brushed her hair away from her ears to reveal tiny diamond studs. "I bought these with the advance from my first book. I always knew I'd be showing them to you one day. Now tell me about your clever daughter and how I saved her life."

18. Autumn Mist

Although Kelsey knew exactly where she was headed, the mist suggested possibilities she hadn't considered. Hinted at surprises, meandering diversions.

Then it became dense fog. Kelsey stopped being sure where she was going. She'd already realised the driving conditions were a good metaphor for her life when red danger signs showed on the gantries above her.

Kelsey left the motorway, found a lay-by and stopped. Going nowhere was better than blindly continuing in the wrong direction.

Kelsey made a call. "Sorry, but due to the weather I won't make my interview this morning."

It was agreed she'd call back if conditions improved and, hopefully, reschedule for later in the day. Meanwhile she had time to think.

She and Lewis used to talk about their plans all the time. Day dreaming it seemed at first, but they'd made much of it work, even things which seemed likely to push them apart. They were quite different in some ways. Kelsey liked to wear smart clothes, drive a car which drew admiring glances and be someone others took notice of. She worked hard and got results.

Lewis wasn't lazy, but lacked her ambition. When they'd first met he ran his graphic design business from his bedsit, almost as a hobby. She'd encouraged him to expand. He'd willingly complied. He reached a point where getting a mortgage together was possible, but he could go no further now without having to employ someone else, get nicer premises than the rented room over the post office. That could happen, but he wouldn't be happy. Such a risk and responsibility would worry him.

Kelsey earned twice Lewis's income and the gap would get wider. If she didn't get the promotion she still hoped to be interviewed for that day, she'd get one soon. They'd be able to buy a bigger house and Lewis could have a home office.

Lewis's job allowed him to be at home for deliveries and getting the washing machine repaired. He did the grocery shopping at quiet times of day, and as his office was just a few minutes from home always had the vacuuming and laundry done, and dinner in the oven by the time she got in. All he did, and his easy-going personality, made her career possible.

Another source of tension early on could have come from his comments about having a family one day.

"That might not be possible, Lewis. I've never been regular and Mum needed IVF to have me."

"You could do the same?"

"Maybe, but I've always assumed I won't have children. I'm not sure I want to."

She'd hoped the two of them would continue as they were indefinitely.

Last week she'd felt different. Unsettled.

"You don't need to go for that promotion," Lewis had said. "We're fine as we are."

"Thanks, but I don't think it's nerves." The job, if she got it, would be a big step up and mean moving house. Of course that could be stressful, but they could handle it between them. She'd take control of all the paperwork and planning, and Lewis would keep her calm and ensure the house became a home.

"Do you feel OK? You certainly look well," he asked.

Physically she felt fine. 'Blooming' was the word which came to mind when she'd seen her reflection that morning. It gave her a clue as to what was going on. But maybe it was excitement about the promotion? That was it, she'd convinced herself and continued the route she'd believed was the one she wanted to travel.

Now she was stuck in a lay-by with time to think. One of the things she thought about was their spare room. If Lewis wanted a home office, why didn't he use that?

"It's for family," he said when she'd asked.

"We don't have visitors often and we could get a sofa bed." It didn't matter anyway. Soon they'd be able to buy somewhere with both a spare room and space for his office.

The fog thinned. Kelsey phoned her potential new boss, who agreed to interview her after lunch. It would be an important discussion, but not the most important. Kelsey drove through the last wisps of mist and found a pharmacy. She bought a pregnancy test kit, which she used in a coffee shop toilet after placing her order for carrot cake and a pot of tea.

Lewis loved carrot cake and frequently tried to convert her. "If I wanted something with vegetables and cheese I'd have ordered quiche," she'd often told him.

Now, for the first time ever, the idea of eating them in cake form appealed. It wasn't a proper diagnosis, but somehow convinced her just as much as seeing the blue lines appear on the test.

She rang Lewis. "Can we talk?"

"Yep, I'm not driving."

"I mean really talk."

"Oh. Is this about the job?"

"It's about you wanting space in our house for family. I think you're about to persuade me you're right."

19. Future Past

"Hello, Juliana," Granddad said, giving her a huge smile, when she called in on the way to her wedding.

"Hello." She couldn't bring herself to call him 'Granddad' anymore. Couldn't bear the confusion that caused. It hurt that although he recognised her, he didn't really know who she was, what they were to each other.

"So, today's the day!" He gestured towards her dress. "You're always a pretty lass, Julianna, but today you're beautiful."

"Thank you." She kissed his cheek.

At least he remembered her name today, that she was a friend of some kind. On bad days he just cried for his darling Eleanor. That was always upsetting, doubly so when Gran was with him. Or, more accurately, Gran was there; Granddad was elsewhere. Sometimes completely lost, sometimes living in the past.

"Why doesn't she come?" he'd cry.

Gran would say, "She's close by and she loves you," as he looked past his wife of fifty years, hoping to see the girl he remembered.

Sometimes other family members tried to bring him into the present. Julianna couldn't. She also longed to return to a time when he was well and strong and frightened of nothing. Granddad woke in the night sometimes, knowing he'd not shut the henhouse door. She couldn't believe he was any less worried after being told the fox he feared was long gone.

When Julianna spoke to Granddad she relived some of her childhood memories along with his. She'd talk of the spring sunshine making the grass grow and the hens lay. She'd tell him about a cow escaping onto a neighbour's tidy lawn, or the healthy twin lambs her favourite sheep had just delivered. Granddad told her of his very earliest memories; evacuated children coming to stay, his mother anxiously reading the newspapers, him bunking off school to go to the cattle market with his uncle. Sometimes he told Julianna about picnicking in the hayfields with her grandmother and the plans they were making.

Before Granddad got ill he'd loved to talk about his youth, it seemed cruel to deny him that pleasure now.

"I'll build that farm up into something I'm proud of and which will keep my family, just you wait and see," Granddad told her time and again.

"Of course you will." How she'd longed to tell him he'd done just that. About the pigpen he'd built himself, his herd of Jersey cows which supplied rich creamy milk to generations of his family. She didn't, because then she'd have to explain why he wasn't still there and had to be kept away from the tractor, pitchforks and wide open spaces for his own safety.

She did tell him about Ben and introduced the two men she loved. Ben described in detail the farm on which he worked. Granddad once ploughed those fertile fields, he'd layered the hedges which still enclosed them, dug the ditches to stop them flooding.

Granddad had congratulated Julianna and Ben and wished them well when told of the engagement.

"I'm going to ask my Eleanor to marry me, just as soon as I get the nerve," he'd confided.

"Good idea," Ben had said. "Then she can help you on the farm, just as Julianna will help me."

Julianna knew she was lucky to have so many happy memories and that both her grandparents were still alive, but it hurt he wasn't coming to her wedding. It would be too upsetting for him now his room in the care home was the only reality he properly recognised.

How could Juliana feel sorry for herself, when she was gaining a husband, not watching him slip away as Gran had to do? It was difficult for Mum too, of course. And for Granddad himself who was so often confused and afraid. Not today, thank goodness. She was pleased about that, wanted it to be enough.

This was her wedding day though, a day on which she'd hoped for a miracle. That always happened in stories and films. One moment of clarity in which he'd recognise her, would understand, would give her his blessing. It hasn't come.

"You remind me of my Eleanor. I hope to see her in a dress like that one day."

"You will, I'm sure."

He had. She didn't dare remind him, show him the photos. Last time anyone had, he'd recognised his beloved, saw she was married but didn't know himself to be the man by her side. He'd cried and cried. They all had. Juliana was glad his treacherous memory had lost that incident too. She mustn't allow herself to think of it now.

"I'd better not keep Ben waiting too long. Wish me luck?"

"I do, not that you'll need it. He's a good man, your Ben."

"He is."

"Have you got something borrowed and something blue, all that? It's lucky and I'm a bit sentimental like."

"Yes, I've borrowed this necklace from my gran." He'd bought it for their twenty-first wedding anniversary. "And the lace for my dress is old, been in the family for years." It was in the picture that upset him so much. "And I'm… er wearing something blue."

His chuckle suggests she doesn't have to explain it's a frilly garter.

"Nothing new, you must have something new." He's getting distressed. That happens sometimes, he gets an idea and must act on it.

He pulls at the drawer in his bedside table, agitated that it won't budge. This was awful. It shouldn't be happening today. It's the very opposite of what she'd hoped for.

At last the drawer comes free and he finds what he wanted.

"Take this."

It's Gran's engagement ring. Often, buying that is one of his last clear memories. Sometimes they went a little further, but never to the point where she accepted it. Seeing how agitated he became when he remembered buying it and couldn't find it, Eleanor took it off and placed it in the drawer. Holding it seemed to comfort him. It allowed him to focus on his hopes for a future that, for everyone else, had been and gone.

"Wear this as your something new. I need it back you know."

"I know and thank you. Thank you so much!" She kisses him again.

Is it her sign? He doesn't really remember her but must care a lot about her happiness to want her to take something so precious. It will do. It will have to do.

The service is beautiful. Perfect except for the one empty seat. Mum walks her down the aisle and places her hand in Ben's. It's a day for looking forward, for making new memories. There are tears, but only happy ones.

As they get ready for the photographer, Julianna shows Gran her own ring. "Granddad lent it to me. I hope you don't mind?"

"Of course not, love. It's right it should be here today."

"It is, but I'd better get it back to him tonight."

Ben is understanding when she says they must visit Granddad after the reception.

"I knew you'd want to see him today."

"I already have." She tells him about her longing for a sign from Granddad and about the loan of the ring.

"I see. Yes, of course we must take it back tonight. I'll tell him to hurry up and ask Eleanor to marry him, so he can be as happy as I am."

Julianna hugs him, so grateful he understands. "He was. I know he was."

"Yes, but there's no harm him having the anticipation all over again, is there?"

"I don't see how there can be."

They take Granddad a slice of their cake and tell him about the day when Juliana returns the ring.

"It's beautiful. I'm sure it brought us luck, and I know Eleanor will love it."

As planned, Ben tells him not to wait too long before proposing.

"I won't and don't you leave it too late to have children. You'll want them to help you on that farm of yours."

"That's true and the grandchildren one day," Ben says.

"We're alike you and I," Granddad says. "Both looking forward to the future. Like you, I want grandchildren one day too. I've heard Juliana here talk about her grandfather, about how much she loves him. I bet he loves her more. Bet he's proud of her." Granddad takes her hand. "I'd be proud to have a granddaughter just like you, my dear." He looks up at Ben, "and I'd like her to marry a man like you."

That is it! Granddad knows of her existence, of her wedding and has given it her blessing. That's what matters, not that for him it is fifty years in the future and to Julianna it's already in the past.

20. Magical Mirror

The first time I looked in Gran's magic mirror I had no idea there was anything unusual about it. I just knew she kept one in her handbag. Quite pretty it was, on the outside anyway. The cover was silver, smooth on the bottom, patterned on the top half with a celtic looking symbol. A tiny hinge and clip allowed it to be opened, then closed again with a satisfying click. In old films where the heroine dabbed powder on her nose and touched up her already flawless matt red lipstick, she used a mirror just like Gran's.

That first time, I was off school with mumps, staying with Gran until the infection passed. That, I was told, was to protect my brothers, but it might have been to save Mum's sanity too – I wasn't a good patient. One reason for that was my age; early teens. My illness had temporarily spoiled how I looked so, to my way of thinking, had completely ruined my life forever.

"Don't be silly, child," Gran had said. "Now, do you think you could eat something?"

My answer was a shake of my head. Chewing hurt and I had little appetite.

"Just hot chocolate then? The doctor did say you need plenty of fluids."

When she went off to make it, I remembered her mirror and wondered whether my face really looked as bad as I feared. It was way worse. I looked like the greediest and ugliest hamster ever!

"Linzie, what are you doing, child?" Gran asked as she returned to find me staring miserably at the horrible swelling.

"Sorry, I didn't think you'd mind me using it." I snapped it shut and held it out.

Gran waved my hand away. "Of course I don't, but if you're going to look in a magic mirror, you have to know how it works."

"Magic?"

"Oh yes. It doesn't show how you look, but how you're seen."

"Aren't they the same thing?"

"Not often. What were you thinking as you looked in it just now?"

"How awful I look."

"But you didn't know how you looked until you opened the mirror, did you?"

"I had a pretty good idea."

"Exactly! You didn't see how you really look, the image in the glass was of how you see yourself."

I guess my puzzlement showed.

"Think about me for a moment. Ready?"

I nodded.

"OK then, look in the mirror again and see how I see you."

That time I saw my whole face. The mumps wasn't gone, but the rest of my face was still pretty. Rather than looking ugly, the swelling looked painful. Of course that's how Gran saw me!

I was about to ask how come Gran had a magic mirror when I remembered Dad once saying Gran was a witch and Mum laughingly telling him to shut up. At the time I'd thought he was teasing…

"Gran, does Dad know about your mirror?"

"Yes, Linzie love. Looking in it gave him the confidence to propose to your mother. You might not exist without it."

Of course that final detail was more than enough to convince me the mirror was very special indeed.

I got over the mumps and later got over being a shallow, vain teenager. The belief that the mirror really was magic remained. Gran encouraged that. Just before a job interview she told me to look in it and see how I'd appear to my potential employers. Somehow the reflection of Gran's cosy living room resembled an open plan office.

"Oh! They'll be seeing if I'd fit in." That might seem obvious now, but until then I'd been thinking about what to wear and memorising my exam grades. By the time I arrived for the interview I was ready to prove I was a pleasant person, and to answer questions in a way which showed I had some idea what would be expected of me and that I was willing to learn how to do it.

A glance in the mirror a few weeks later showed that the colleague I thought disliked me was actually intimidated by my confidence. The next time I made a small mistake I asked for her help in putting it right and we've been friends ever since.

Over the years, I tried thinking of my boyfriends and looking in the mirror. Once my hand was damp and the mirror slipped a little to show just my cleavage. Another time I realised how much the frilled blouse I wore made me look like a maid. Once my attention was drawn to the car keys I'd placed on the coffee table. None of those relationships lasted long.

When I'd been dating Alex long enough that I thought he might be the one, I wanted to know how he saw me. I didn't get an answer as only a shaft of sunlight was reflected… or did that mean he was completely dazzled by me? That was how I felt about him – even while trying to look through the brilliant light for my own face, it was his image in my mind's eye.

I introduced him to Gran and asked if he could try the mirror.

"Good idea, child."

She made sure Alex had one of the comfortable chairs, insisted he accept tea and cake, and eventually handed him the mirror. "You think of Linzie, then open it up."

He did as instructed. "Wow, that sun is strong!"

Gran adjusted the curtain and told him to try again.

"That's better, I can see myself properly now – and why she says I'm good looking!" He grinned, as though only joking.

If the mirror really did show how we were seen, that meant Alex saw me as dazzled by his good looks and what he saw in me was… not really me at all, but someone dazzled by his good looks.

Gran shook her head and told him, "You don't see how you look, but how Linzie sees you."

"Same thing," Alex said.

"You're probably right," Gran admitted. She seemed sad.

I thought about that for a long time. Did she mean the mirror wasn't really magic? Alex certainly thought it was ordinary. In that case what had I seen each time I'd looked in it?

When I had the mumps, I'd been worried about the swelling, so that's all I'd seen. When Gran told me to think of her and look again, I saw the bigger picture – literally and figuratively. Perhaps thinking how boyfriends and colleagues thought of me allowed details from my subconscious to come to the surface.

Looking at my reflection before the job interview I'd focussed on what was important and thought I'd seen a computer monitor, pile of paperwork and busy office. In reality it must have been Gran's TV, stack of magazines and chaotically patterned curtains.

Those curtains had been open when I'd tried to discover how Alex saw me. When he'd looked in the mirror he was sitting in the same spot – Gran had made sure of that. We'd both been dazzled by sunlight so not seen much. That was equally true away from the mirror. Alex hadn't bothered to see below the pretty surface to the real me and I'd not seen deeper than his good looks because there was nothing more.

The mirror is mine now. I no longer think it's magic, but I treasure it as a gift from someone I loved, and as a beautiful object. I carry it in my handbag just as Gran always did, so I had it on me when Paul took me out for a romantic meal. As we waited for dessert he seemed a little uncomfortable and mentioned he'd been teased about his bald spot.

"You're not going bald," I assured him and gave him the mirror to check.

I laughed as he tried looking at the back of his head to see the patch without hair. He looked funny doing it, but I also caught a glimpse of bare skin in the mirror. Until then I'd not noticed anything about him which could be considered any kind of imperfection. At last I'd seen him as he truly was – a man who might well lose his hair at an early age, but who was truly perfect to me.

"What's so funny?" Paul asked.

"My gran said the mirror was magic and I think maybe she was right after all."

"How does it work then?"

"You think of someone, then when you look at your reflection you don't see how you really look, but as how they see you."

"That should be easy as, well, I think of you all the time, Linzie."

"Go on then, look."

He opened the mirror again and grinned. "I can't see a bald spot from here! Actually I look OK."

"Yes, you do, more than OK actually."

"Your turn." He handed it over.

I thought of the man I loved and opened the mirror. I saw myself of course, but the candlelight, gleaming cutlery and crystal glasses added another reflection. It was of the dainty gypsophila flowers in the vase and my folded linen napkin on the table. The combined effect made it look as though I were wearing a simply white dress and a delicate veil, just like the one in Gran's wedding photo.

When I looked back at Paul he'd left his seat to kneel at my side and was offering me a beautiful diamond ring. Ever since then, whenever I've looked in Gran's mirror I've not only seen my own reflection, but that of Paul. There's nothing unusual about that, it's simply that we're always together… and that really is magic.

21. The Mirrored Gates

At first the man thought he was waking up. Then he was sure he must be dreaming about walking towards those huge, iridescent gates. Gradually something came to him, not quite memories but an awareness, and he realised he was dead.

He stopped walking. Being dead was a shock. He'd always known it would happen of course, he wasn't a stupid man, yet somehow he hadn't expected it to. He'd made a will, but hadn't truly considered that the world would cease to have him in it. Perhaps nobody did.

He'd been involuntarily walking towards the gates, but had halted his progress when he realised what was happening. Could he turn back? He found he couldn't. Could he take a different direction? He could not. What he could do was continue towards the gates, so he did that – very slowly. Then more quickly. They were the pearly gates. Of course they were. He was going to heaven!

As the man drew nearer, he could see through the gates to the world which lay beyond. It looked very like the one in which he'd lived. That was odd. Never having completely believed in heaven, he'd given little thought to how it might look, but this definitely wasn't right. Shouldn't there be more light? And angels. Lost loved ones eager to greet him. Gentle rivers flowing with milk and honey. Or did he mean ambrosia, whatever that was.

There was someone walking towards him. St Peter? If it was, he didn't live up to expectation either. No long flowing robes and shiny halo. No huge bunch of keys. Not even a beard. But then nobody back on earth would have actually seen St Peter, would they? Why shouldn't he look like a perfectly ordinary man?

What would happen now? Would he be let straight in? Have to give his name and wait for it to be checked off a list? Perhaps he'd be asked questions, to prove his right to entry. That would be fine.

He was a good person. Not a murderer or sadist. He wasn't racist, hadn't tortured animals or started wars. He'd never hurled abuse at people who were different from him. All his life he'd worked hard, played hard, striven to be the best he could be. He'd done well, earning not just money, but power, position and respect. Even so, he walked a little slower.

St Peter, if it was he, slowed too, as though sensing his hesitation. The man took another step. So did the person on the other side of the gates. A mirror! The gates were a giant mirror. Sort of.

That world beyond wasn't exactly like the world as he'd left it. Everything and everywhere seemed to be happening at once. There was his school, with children playing outside. His house and his holiday home on the coast. The offices in which he'd worked, restaurants where he'd eaten, the tailors from which he bought his suits. There was the home in which he'd grown up, and the car in which he'd died.

This wasn't the whole world, but his world. Was heaven an endless replay of life? Perhaps he'd get to choose which bits he relived? He concentrated on the schoolyard and events which had happened there. They'd been good days, he supposed. They'd certainly set him up for life, although that was as much from the useful contacts he made there, as any lessons he'd learned. He heard the shouts and laughter of the boys playing conkers, felt the shoelace in his own hand, wound tight, ready for him to strike.

Before he could see if it was a match he'd won, he was in the classroom, being instructed in Latin. The master had barely begun to lecture them on conjugating verbs before the man was in the dining hall, with a full plate in front of him. The child who was him wouldn't eat straight away, he'd have to wait until grace was said. What an appropriate memory to have outside the pearly gates. Would that be enough for St Peter to let him in?

Only it wasn't St Peter waiting beyond those gates, but the reflection of himself. Could it be that he was his own judge? In a way that made sense; nobody knows us better than we do ourselves. Weirdly the man began to feel nervous. There was nothing he could do now but continue, although it seemed he could dictate the speed.

As he got nearer the gates, his own image swelled, to fill almost the whole view of what lay beyond. He'd been told once that he thought the whole world was all about him, existed for his benefit, and everyone and everything else was secondary to him. In truth he'd been told words to that effect more than once. Repetition didn't make them true.

OK, maybe he had been a little what some would call egotistical, but he'd had a right to be. He was somebody. He'd worked hard always. Nobody had given him handouts or special treatment. In fact sometimes promotions, chances or rewards which should have been his had gone to someone else. Someone no better qualified, but better connected, or who offered something towards the company's diversity targets.

The man hadn't put up with that unfairness. He'd set up on his own, with no help from anyone. Just the money from his parents, which would have come to him anyway, had he outlived them. Once or twice he'd been lucky with investments or in securing contracts, through friends who'd brought him into a good deal. He'd always scrupulously returned those favours. That's how these things worked.

The image from beyond the gates began to swirl and dissolve. Just for a moment there was nothing. He understood then. What he'd seen wasn't his own reflection superimposed onto the sight of heaven beyond. Everything he'd seen was in some way a vision of things he'd experienced. The actuality of his life flashing before his eyes. He still had no idea what heaven looked like. That probably didn't matter – he was going there anyway and was almost within touching distance of the gates.

The images on the gates had changed. They still displayed the world as he'd known it, but the individual examples weren't ones he recognised as being connected with his life. The school was different. Bigger, but poorer. The streets were narrower, the houses smaller and more crowded. There was less of everything, except people. Though greater in number, they too seemed less than the people who'd lived in the man's world.

The man was no longer alone. Walking towards him was a vicar. Or priest or minister or something. Wait, was he an imam? A rabbi? Whoever he was drew nearer, yet although there was no doubt that he was some type of cleric or religious person, neither his creed nor even the colour of his skin was apparent. How could that be? People were often advised to look beyond such things, but in life it had proved impossible for the man to ignore the evidence of his own eyes.

The cleric kept walking towards the man. No; it was the gates he approached. That life being displayed must be his. Yes, he was smiling, recognising it, and himself. Then the cleric stopped, and reached out to the man.

"Are you ready?" the cleric asked.

"You're St Peter?"

"I'm no saint, just an ordinary man who has done his best."

The man understood the words, though they were not English. Or rather, not just English. And though he heard 'saint' he knew it stood for prophet, avatar and so much more.

The man looked at the images playing on the gates, and saw this cleric talking to all those people. Speaking with those in need and offering more than words of comfort. He provided hope and relief, brought about reconciliation. It wasn't all talk either. He fed the hungry, not nearly all, but as many as he was able. When he could, he provided shelter, eased loneliness, restored self worth.

"I'm not sure I am ready, but you are," the man said. There was no doubt in his mind that this… this person of faith, whatever that may be, deserved his place in heaven.

"Thank you," the cleric said. He turned and walked towards the gates.

As they swung open, the man saw that he'd been right the first time, it was a vicar who stepped through. Just for a moment the world beyond was visible. The man looked into heaven. A fabulous cathedral, with sunshine streaming through the stained glass windows, bathing the congregation in a holy light. The people beyond reached out to the new arrival, welcoming him. Then the gates swung shut.

That was OK then. Heaven was a Christian place and the man had been baptised. He'd said his prayers at school and celebrated Christmas. Yet he doubted. That cleric had been a Christian as he approached the gates and when he stepped through them, but in the period between those times it wasn't his beliefs which had played out on the screen, but his actions.

The man looked again at the gates, which had reverted to showing his own life. He didn't waste time looking for scenes like those he'd witnessed from the cleric's life. He'd not helped wherever he could.

Phrases such as, 'we should help our own first,' 'donations don't reach those who need it most,' and 'nobody gives me handouts,' echoed in his mind. He'd used those and others to avoid dipping into his considerable assets, seeing no contradiction until now. There were times he'd made what he'd told the tax man were charitable donations, but they'd been to make him look good, or extend the bar at the golf club.

The images on the gates swirled again and the man saw a woman approaching. Not a pretty woman, nor the member of any board of directors, nor even a teacher or nurse. The kind of person he wouldn't have noticed had it not been just the two of them outside the gates to heaven.

She stopped a pace behind the man, as though deference to someone like him was natural to her. Both of them looked up at the gates. Her school was there – a poorly funded state school she could rarely attend, as she was carer to her younger siblings. The mother was probably feckless, the kind of person who'd take benefits intended for her children, and buy gin and lottery tickets. Most likely someone who didn't properly clean her council house and let junk moulder on the weedy patch in front of it. The kind of person those the man voted for had said couldn't be helped, so made no effort to try. The money was better off spent elsewhere. Somewhere decent people like the man would benefit.

More of the woman's life was revealed. She had a job. Two jobs. Not important, profitable ones like the man's. For her, hard work didn't mean putting her expensive education to use, and schmoozing her influential cronies, but scrubbing floors, mind numbing hours on a production line, mending clothes, stretching meals. She did all she could and it wasn't nearly enough.

Her kids looked like they ran wild. Maybe they did when their mother could get overtime. They looked like the free school meals weren't enough to fill their bellies. Their mother's choice was to leave them alone, or leave them hungry.

The woman was… The man tried to stop himself thinking of the words he'd used to describe people like her. Attempted to put aside the times he could have voted differently, invested in community schemes instead of offshore. Treated the women who cleaned his office, served him in the supermarket and ironed his shirts, with respect.

It was far too little, far too late, but he stepped aside and politely said, 'after you', just like the gentleman he'd always told himself he was.

She looked surprised, but thanked him and walked up to the gates. When they swung open for her the man glimpsed what was beyond. No towering cathedral now, but an ordinary home. Nowhere near as large or nice as the houses the man had lived in, but it looked clean and comfortable. He was sure it would be warm and the fridge full of food.

There were people in the house. Crowded together and reaching welcoming arms to the woman. The gates swung shut.

Time passed. The man stood still. He'd always thought he'd spent his life getting ahead, but now he wondered. The images on the gates swirled, the view of the world changed, and another person approached. Neither man nor woman, in the man's opinion, but an it in a skirt and heels, too much make-up and stubble. Long hair, big hands and an Adam's apple.

The gates showed their world had been full of confusion, inside themselves and in those who loved them. They'd had hopes and dreams very like his own had been. They too had worked and ate and slept. Walked, talked, read, watched… Around all of that were hurdles and hatred. They'd tried to fit in, but hadn't often been allowed to. The man had never yelled insults at people like them, but neither had he stood between them and abuse. He hadn't marched with them. Had barely considered them people.

Somewhere on the screen the man saw the person write their name. The one they'd given themselves. It didn't suit the six-foot broad shouldered human being he saw in front of him, but it was a pretty name which might be perfect for the person they were inside.

"You go ahead, Jessica," the man said.

The person, she, Jessica, smiled. No. She grinned. Beamed.

She was outside the gates of heaven, yet him making the tiny effort to address her in the way she preferred, indicating his acceptance of her right to exist as the person she declared herself to be, had brought her joy. He could easily have brought many others a little happiness on Earth with a kind word or thoughtful gesture. Could have. Should have.

When the gates swung open for Jessica, the man saw the world just as he knew it. A world where he'd always been accepted exactly as he was. Where he'd walked without fear. Didn't have to prove his right to exist, to succeed, to be happy. A world he'd always thought was fair, but now saw had been nothing of the sort.

He waited and watched as others approached the gates, recognised themselves and saw their lives. The man witnessed things they'd suffered, and their acts of charity, kindness, humanity. He saw a glimpse of what heaven would be like for them.

Campaigners who stepped through into a world of ancient woodland and clean seas, or one free of nuclear bombs, or where every child had food to eat, and books they could read. People who'd tried in life and failed through no fault of their own were rewarded with success. Those whose bodies had in life been ravaged by pain or disease, or whose functions were limited by disabilities, stepped whole and healthy into a world of freedom. So did those wrongly convicted, or imprisoned for their beliefs or sexuality.

So many people. So many differences. So many obstacles which had been battled. So many attempts to help. Nothing which reflected the man's life. And so many versions of heaven. None he wanted. None he deserved.

Every time someone stepped through the gates there were people beyond, stretching out hands in welcome. Would anyone be waiting for the man? And how long had it taken to think of anyone but himself? He'd cared about what awaited him, but not what had happened to loved ones who'd gone before. Or rather those he should have loved, instead of thinking of no one but himself.

There were those left behind too. If he'd spared them a thought it was envy that they still lived. They might be grieving. Yes, shallow as he'd been, he had also been loved. He didn't want people to grieve for him. He'd like them to think instead of the life he'd lived, and to go on with theirs, making it the best it could be. The best for themselves, yes – but for others too. He didn't want them waiting outside these gates, seeing themselves for what they truly were, and being dismayed.

If he continued to wait outside these gates, he'd see more people approach. Learn their lives had not been like his. Perhaps, deep down, he'd always known he was free from disadvantages. Now he saw it as others did, how it had really been – he'd had advantages. Been lucky, privileged. Maybe if he waited long enough, he'd see people who'd had it better than he had, but not much better and there wouldn't be many of them.

The man wondered what his heaven, the one he was now sure he wouldn't be granted, might be like. Slowly he realised it would exactly mirror the life he'd lived. A life which had provided all he needed and wanted. The one he'd complained of, because others had as much, or nearly as much. The life he'd never properly appreciated, as he'd always been searching for more.

If his life had been heaven, what lay on the other side of those gates must be something else. Something he deserved.

He had learned a great deal as he'd waited outside. Enough to grant him a second chance? He wasn't entirely sure that was the case, and horribly afraid his guess that he was his own version of St Peter, his own judge, was correct. There was nothing he could do now, but walk closer to the gates. As he got nearer, his own image swelled to fill almost the whole view of what had been his world.

The gates swung open and the man stepped through.

22. Working Magic

"Aunty Wendy, are you a wizard?" Toby asked as I walked him home from school.

"A wizard?"

"Someone who can do magic spells like making things disappear or turn into frogs."

"No love, I'm not a wizard."

"Girls can be," he coaxed. "Hermione is one, and there's Winnie the Witch. I like her."

I had no idea who Hermione might be. "Some people might say I'm a witch, I expect, but I'm not one of those either."

"You don't do any magic at all?" Toby made that sound very odd indeed.

"No, none."

"Then they probably just say you're a witch because you dress funny and are a bit odd and have a big nose."

Kids! Got to love their honesty, haven't you? "I expect you're right," I agreed. We were back at my place by then, so I poured him a glass of milk and tipped a few biscuits onto a plate. That wasn't magic, but it seemed a minor miracle I had those items and both were perfectly fresh.

"Do you know any magic?" I asked Toby as the reason for the conversation gradually dawned on me.

"Yes. I'll show you!"

He did. He wasn't very good, but he tried really hard and kept me entertained for quite a while.

"He was no trouble at all," I was able to tell his mum when she came to collect him. I'm Hayley's aunt really; Toby's great aunt. Thankfully he doesn't call me that – I don't feel nearly ancient enough for the title. Actually he'd sort of referred to me as a girl, albeit an oddly dressed one with a big nose. The thought made me smile.

Hayley must have caught my expression as she looked relieved. "Same time tomorrow, then?"

"Yes, looking forward to it." I actually was. I couldn't remember the last time I'd been looking forward to anything, not in the way that phrase is usually meant. I'd been anticipating collecting Toby from school, but I'd been looking forward to it with dread.

For one thing, I didn't go out much and the idea of walking down the street and mixing with all those parents, grandparents, and what have you, outside the school gates had given me panic attacks. That seemed silly, so I kept it to myself. Of course that meant I couldn't tell Hayley why I was so reluctant. She'd explained she'd been asked by the magazine she worked for to stand in for the features editor who was having an operation. It was her big chance. If she could show she could do the job short term, but with full time hours, there was the chance she'd be offered the post permanently when the other person retired in a couple of years. By then Toby would be at secondary school… but for a couple of weeks now she needed someone to collect him after school and keep him safe until quarter to six.

I knew how much she wanted her name on the list of editors, and how much they could do with the extra pay just then, even if that's all she got out of standing in. It wasn't as though I was too busy to help out. I'd reluctantly offered to do it if she couldn't find anyone else.

Thankfully the school wouldn't just let anyone fetch a child. Sensible policy of course, but I appreciated the fact for myself. Hayley had to introduce me to his teachers and we decided the best way to do that was to collect him together on the Thursday and Friday of the week before I'd do it myself. With Hayley by my side I coped. That gave me the weekend to fret over looking after Toby. I didn't know much about children and I wasn't making a great job of looking after myself. I looked odd because I'd not had my hair cut, or bought new clothes, for years and that's because I rarely went out. The reason I didn't go out… well I don't know, I just couldn't face it.

Picking up Toby went without a hitch, and so did caring for him. I don't usually have much food in. The nearest supermarket opens 24 hours, so I'd gone when it was quiet and stocked up on cakes, biscuits, milk and juice. Hayley had said not to worry about feeding him his tea but he might like a snack.

Thanks to his magic tricks the time flew by and I forgot to ask if he had any homework until it was nearly time to go, but we did run through the words he was supposed to learn.

"You can't do magic, Aunty Wendy, but you can do spelling!"

After he'd gone I thought about his magic tricks. It hadn't mattered he wasn't very good and needed practice. Maybe the same was true of my childminding? I'd made an effort to tidy up the house. I doubted Toby noticed, but Hayley had. She didn't actually say anything, but I saw her surprised glance into the now hygienic kitchen and the living room with space for Toby to sit without moving anything first.

As I walked to collect him on the Tuesday, I wondered why he'd asked me the question he did. I'd not been joking about people calling me a witch, but I doubted that's what he meant and I thought there'd been more behind it than wanting to show me his tricks. He's a very precise sort of child. Wizard is what he'd said, so wizard was what he meant, not magician or conjurer.

There was an obvious way to find out; I asked him. "Why did you think I might be a wizard, Toby?"

"Because you used to live in a cupboard under the stairs like Harry Potter."

At least I understood who Hermione was then, but not much else. "I don't live in a cupboard, Toby. I have a normal bedroom upstairs." Admittedly there were so many things piled on the stairs they didn't look as though they were used much.

"Now you do, but didn't you use to live under the stairs?"

"No, never."

"Oh." He looked thoughtful for a moment. Then happy. "So can I see your skeleton?"

"Skeleton?"

"It's all the bones people have in them." He got me to feel his fingers and count the three bones in each.

I admitted to having bones in my own body.

"I know you have, Aunty Wendy. You're just skin and bone," he explained kindly and patiently. "I didn't mean those ones, but the skeleton you keep in your wardrobe."

My housekeeping skills aren't great, but even so he seemed to have odd ideas about the uses I put my cupboards to. "Why do you think I would do that?"

"Mum said. It's a bit complicated."

"OK." I tried to look capable of understanding.

"Dad said you used to live under the stairs but not any more." He frowned in concentration. "He said you should come out of the closet."

"He did?"

"Yes, but Mum said you'd never been in one and he hadn't been listening to her."

"Your mum was right."

"That's what I just worked out which is why I knew you must have a skeleton in your wardrobe."

"Ah." Obviously he'd half heard and a quarter understood his parent's conversation about me.

"It's not an actual skeleton," I said.

"More like a picture?"

"Yes." Maybe that was a cowardly reply, but I didn't want to explain my metaphorical skeleton in the cupboard to Toby.

"Can I see it?"

"Not today. How about you teach me one of your magic tricks?"

When he'd gone, I thought back to my skeleton. I once killed someone. I don't mean I murdered them and they're buried under the patio, to be dug up for Toby's amusement. It was an accident. I've accepted that now though I blamed myself for a long time. I'd been driving with my fiancé and we got a puncture and crashed. Not my fault. Not anyone's, but I barely had a bruise and he was dead. It took me a long time to get over it. I managed to get myself run over a year or so later. OK, exactly a year later. Doctors thought it was attempted suicide. It wasn't, I just hadn't cared enough about myself to look both ways when stepping out into the road. I was diagnosed with depression and given pills. They made me tired and didn't help so I stopped taking them.

X-rays! I'd had-X rays taken. When I left hospital I was given a whole pile of paperwork. I'd not looked at it, but I supposed the X-rays would be included. Toby might like to see them. I started looking that evening, but I soon realised that in order to find anything I'd need to start chucking things out. It didn't take me long to fill the recycling bin with free newspapers and adverts for half price pizzas. One of those charity bags had been pushed through my door the previous week and as luck would have it was due to be collected the next morning. I filled it with clothes so out of date even I didn't wear them. Nothing of his, the man's who'd once lived here with me.

I shook away my memories and filled a bin bag with books and other bits and pieces I hoped might raise a few pennies. If I left them together with the charity bag they'd be taken, wouldn't they?

My neighbour spotted me putting them out the next morning. "Having a clear out?" she asked. I couldn't fail to hear the hopeful tone.

I nodded and turned to rush back in. As I did I saw the house through her eyes. Porch piled high with junk, things stacked on the windowsills, unkempt front garden. "A lot of it's just rubbish though, no good for the charity shops," I found myself admitting.

"There's never much in my bins, fill them up if you like."

"Thanks." I did. I didn't stop until it was time to fetch Toby.

As I walked back with him, the person two doors down said that if there was any space in their bin I was welcome to make use of it.

"Thanks, I will."

"Having a clear out always makes me feel better," she said.

"You've found your stairs!" Toby said when we went in.

"Yes. I was looking for my skeleton."

"Have you found it yet?"

"No. I'll have to throw out lots more things first."

"I can help." Toby was excellent at sorting things into recycling and non recycling piles and carrying them round to neighbours' bins. They teach about recycling at school and he was confident of a big green sticker after doing so much.

We hardly had time to talk, so it wasn't until the next day he said, "Are you ill, Aunty Wendy?"

"I'm fine love. Why do you ask?" I was surprised, as for the first time in ages I'd slept well.

"Your neighbour said doing the clearing up would make you feel better."

"Oh, yes. Well, she was right, it's working." To be honest I'm sure his cheerful company was making the difference.

"So I'm helping?"

"Yes. Definitely."

"Shall we do more tidying?"

We couldn't really as I'd been at it all day and every bin on the street was now full. I'd have to wait until they were emptied and in any case, it didn't seem fair to have him do my housework.

"How about I help you with something today?" I suggested.

I'd imagined us struggling through his maths homework, but he wanted me to kick footballs at him in the park so he could practise saving goals. My feeble efforts can't have done much to improve his skills, but they seemed to help his confidence and that's important too, isn't it?

After the two weeks were up I dreaded going back to my pre Toby routine. It was almost funny to remember that only a short time before I'd dreaded walking down to the school to get him and there I was almost tearful at the thought of not doing it again.

I had a reprieve. Hayley's colleague was not yet fit enough to return to work.

"Don't worry, I'd be happy to collect Toby for another week," I assured his mum.

"Really?"

"Yes. He's doing me the power of good."

"I am pleased and I don't just mean for me."

"No, I didn't think so."

"Wendy… will you think about going back to the doctor?"

"All right."

She hugged me. We'd argued before when she'd tried to persuade me to seek help, but maybe she'd been right to be concerned about me since Brian… since the accident.

I honestly did think about making an appointment but decided I was fine.

On my extra week with Toby I found the paperwork from the hospital. Unfortunately there were no X-rays amongst it. Not wanting to disappoint Toby, I went to the library in the hope of getting a book. I had to register first, but once I was a member there was no problem about borrowing a whole stack of books illustrated with X-rays and drawings of bones.

Toby wasn't too impressed until I explained that I'd had photos of my skeleton taken because I'd smashed it up. He held the books up against the appropriate limbs and felt my arm, which had been the worst damaged, but could find no trace of damage until I rolled up my sleeve to show him the scars.

"The doctor made everything OK?"

"Eventually, yes. I had to have operations." I'd spoken to Hayley on the phone and she'd said it was fine to give him all the gory details.

"Horrible child loves all that stuff, just as long as he doesn't get the idea it's about to happen to him."

"More than one operation?" Toby asked.

"Yes. The doctor didn't get it quite right the first time."

Hayley was right. He seemed particularly delighted with the part about me having to have it re-broken because it hadn't set quite straight. I explained about the anaesthetic meaning it didn't hurt.

"Thank you for showing me your skeleton, Aunty Wendy. It's good I saw it, but I'm a little bit sad I won't be coming here after school any more."

I assured him the feeling was mutual. "You can come other times. Maybe Mum will have to work late occasionally or something."

I got through the weekend, but on Monday morning when I awoke to the realisation I wouldn't be collecting Toby that afternoon so had no reason to go out, or get dressed or even crawl out of bed, I hit a real slump. What brought me back was the bins being emptied.

My neighbour came round and banged on the door until I answered. "Oh sorry, I didn't realise you were having a lie-in," she said when I staggered down.

"It's OK, I was awake."

"I just wanted to say the bins are emptied and you can carry on filling them. Mine and Jo's at 37 and that chap's at 39 anyway. I haven't asked anyone else, but I don't suppose they'll mind."

"Oh, right. Thanks."

She looked past me into the much improved, but still quite cluttered, hallway. "Time to start again!"

Maybe I should have been annoyed with her interference, but I couldn't be bothered to care. I didn't think I could be bothered to start again with the clear out either, but what else did I have to do?

All week I worked. By then all the actual rubbish was gone and I was left with cleaning, sorting out things I no longer wanted from those I did, and everything of Brian's. One day I put on one of his sweaters. As I pulled it on over my head I remembered wearing it before. He'd wanted to walk up the hill and watch the fireworks, but I'd said it would be too cold. Brian never let me get away with such feeble excuses to have fun and wrapped me up in so many layers I was toasty warm even before we reached the bonfire.

I had bouts of frantic activity and bouts of sitting on the now clutter-free stairs and sobbing. The sobbing wasn't unusual, not for me those last few years, but my three weeks with Toby had shown me it wasn't inevitable. He'd taught me a lot with those questions of his. Including the fact that although the doctors had no trouble diagnosing my broken bones, they'd needed more than one attempt at treatment. The diagnosis of depression wouldn't have been quite so obvious, but I supposed my GP had got it right. He'd not done so well with the first attempt at treatment, but there might be a better alternative. I rang and made an appointment.

Then I called Hayley and told her.

"I am pleased. How about coming over for Sunday lunch?" She'd invited me lots of times in the past, but I'd never wanted to put her to the trouble. This time though, she persuaded me to accept, by craftily saying Toby would be pleased to see me.

Over roast chicken and mashed potatoes, I asked Hayley about the situation at the magazine. She told me the current features editor had decided to take early retirement.

"That's good news isn't it? You will be offered her job?"

"I already have."

"Excellent. You must be pleased to have that settled. Will you start as soon as Toby goes to secondary school?"

It wasn't quite such good news apparently. The person in question wanted to leave much sooner than that and if Hayley couldn't accept the position almost immediately then the magazine would have to give it to someone else.

The solution seemed pretty obvious to me. "Well, take it now then. You're ready, aren't you?"

"I am, but…" She nodded towards Toby.

"She means I'm not going to the next school for ages and ages," Toby helpfully explained.

The solution there seemed obvious too. "Then I'll be collecting you for ages and ages."

"We can't ask you to do that," Toby's dad said, but I heard the hope in his voice.

"You're not asking, I'm offering. I'd like to do it."

"Cool, then I can show you more magic tricks," Toby said. "I learned a new one last week."

"Well, if you're sure…" Hayley said.

"That's settled then," I said. "Toby can come to me and work some more of his magic." I was sure the combined efforts of him and my GP would do the trick.

23. What Granny Knew

"I wonder what we'll get," Chloe said.

The five cousins waited to be shown into the office of the lady who was once Granny's neighbour, and was now the executor of her will. At Granny's request, they were assembling on what would have been her 96th birthday, to receive her last gift to each of them.

It didn't matter to Emily. Nothing which Granny could have left her would in any way compensate for the loss of the woman who'd loved her so much, and been loved just as much in return.

Emily wasn't an only child like her cousins Jack and Chloe. She wasn't the eldest child in her family, that was her sister Megan. Nor was she the youngest of them all, her brother Thomas had that privilege. Amongst her family or at school she'd never been the tallest or shortest, cleverest, fastest or slowest. Emily didn't stand out for any reason.

She was ordinary to everyone but Granny. Her grandmother had made her feel special. Not more special than her siblings and cousins perhaps, but as though she were truly valued as a unique individual.

"Granny always gave us nice presents," Megan said.

Yes, she had. That was because she loved them, because she knew them so well, and put a great deal of thought into giving them something they really wanted. Even when it had been cash or a voucher, that was for a good reason, not simply to make things easier for Granny.

"It's not going to be a lot, so don't get your hopes up," Thomas said. "The house has already been signed over to our parents and she didn't have much else."

'She had love,' Emily wanted to say. 'And she gave it all to us.' Suddenly that thought gave her comfort, like one of Granny's cuddles.

"Whatever it is, I bet we all get the same," was Megan's opinion. "Granny was always fair."

Yes, she'd been fair, but that didn't mean giving them all the same. If any of them fell, Granny cleaned their grazes and applied ointment. They all got cuddles and kisses. Some also got a lollipop, while others were gently told off for being reckless.

"That's true," Thomas said. "Our Christmas and birthday presents were all worth the same amount."

Why could none of them see that Granny gave them so much more than could be bought with money? It wasn't that the others hadn't loved Granny. Their tears at her funeral a few months previously would have proved that, had Emily ever doubted it. They just hadn't needed her like Emily did. They weren't ordinary.

Thomas had started a part time job while still at school, been taken on full time the day he left and now at seventeen was already in line for promotion. Megan was doing really well in her career too, as was Jack. Chloe, who'd got married just a few weeks before Emily, ran her own business. Emily didn't have a career – she had a job. One she would soon have to give up.

"Sorry to have kept you waiting," the executor said. "Please come in now." She gestured for them to go ahead of her.

As Emily, neither first nor last, stepped into the room she saw a polished wooden table on which rested five square boxes. Each was covered in a differently patterned sheet of wrapping paper.

"Your grandmother said you'd know which was yours," the lady said.

Thomas took a seat behind the box covered with bold black and white stripes. Megan opted for the pattern of flowers and vegetables. Jack's was decorated with cakes, and Chloe's with glitter. That left the plain blue one for Emily. It was her favourite colour, but compared with the others it seemed ordinary. Suddenly Emily remembered an old shoe box stuffed with papers, and realised there was something of Granny's she'd like.

"You may open them now," they were told.

Thomas went first. His box held cash which he counted. "That's weird… you know that promotion I mentioned? I need to pass my driving test to get it. Now I can afford an intensive course."

"I don't see what's weird about that," Jack said. "It's what you need, so it's what Granny gave you."

"It's not enough to pay for the entire course. Don't get me wrong, I'm not complaining. It's a lot of money so I've been saving every penny I can. With Granny's money on top, it's pretty much the exact amount."

Chloe's box contained Granny's strings of beads, and a few brooches. All the girls had played with them as kids, Chloe more than most. Maybe they'd encouraged her to set up her mail order jewellery design and repair business?

As Chloe rummaged through the box, Emily saw her give a tiny frown, then shake her head. "Talking of weird… I've been offered the chance to display my work in a gallery," Chloe said. "I'd love to but didn't have enough stock to keep some of it tied up that way. I can clean and repair these and put them on show with a few I've made."

"That's good, but I wouldn't call it weird. I'm sure we all guessed her jewellery would come to you."

Emily and the others nodded their agreement with Jack.

"Yeah, it's not a huge surprise," Chloe said absentmindedly. "Anyone recognise this?" she showed them a bangle with 'sweetheart' engraved on it.

"I do," Megan said. "Except I thought it had her name on."

"So did I. Doesn't matter though. There's some great stuff here – or there will be with a little work."

Jack opened his box."It's like she knew more than she could have," he whispered.

"Knew what, Jack?" Chloe asked. "Are you admitting to weirdness?"

"Not exactly. But yeah, I do admit it's amazing how well she knew us. Uncanny." He showed them Granny's recipe books. Some passed down from her own grandmother, some much newer. They were all well used. Most had multiple notes for adaptations ranging from tips for managing without meat, eggs and anything else hard to come by during rationing, to feeding faddy grandchildren including one with an allergy.

"I've been trying to persuade my boss that if the restaurant catered for people with special dietary needs we'd get more customers as well as providing a service. He said I could try, but only if the food was truly interesting – not the same vegan or gluten free dishes you can get anywhere."

"Let's see if she had the same insight into my life," Megan said. She reached into her box and held up a rusty key. "For her shed?" she guessed.

"That's right," the executor confirmed. "It's the contents she wanted you to have."

For the first time Emily doubted the wisdom of Granny's choice. Megan used to love helping Granny in the garden, but now didn't have time to tend more than a few pots on the balcony of her modern flat. These days Megan's nails were as immaculate as her business suits.

Megan held the key in her hand and stared at it, shaking her head. "Like Jack said, it's as if she knew. She can't have because I've never told anyone."

"Never told anyone what?" Chloe demanded.

"Tell us now," Jack coaxed.

"I know everyone is so proud of me with my important job in the city, but I hate it."

Jack and Chloe looked stunned.

"But you're doing so well," Thomas said.

"You're going to give it up?" Emily guessed.

"I've been thinking about it for a while. I only made up my mind while I was sitting with Granny towards the end. I talked about helping her in the garden when I was little. I didn't tell her my decision though." Megan looked over at the lady solicitor. "When did Granny arrange for us to have these boxes?"

"She told me her idea several months ago, and said how she'd liked them wrapped, but it was just before she went into hospital that I had the final instructions about what to place in them."

"That's what I thought. She can't have known what would help us most, yet somehow she did."

"I get that for me, Chloe and Tomas," Jack said, but you don't really want all the junk out of Granny's shed do you, Megs?"

"Not all of it, no. Just her garden tools. They were good quality and have decades of use left in them. I've decided to train as a garden designer, and using them will make it seem as if I'm working alongside Granny once again."

"What's in your box, Emily?" Thomas asked.

"Granny's school report cards," she said, then took off the lid to find what she'd hoped would be in there. Emily read out the matron's assessment, 'Miss Boswell is perfectly normal in all respects.' She recited the grades – 'average' in every subject. Then Emily read few of the comments, which all boiled down to, 'Helena is a pleasant but quite ordinary girl.'

"Granny wasn't average, she was amazing!" Chloe said.

"Normal and ordinary make it sound like she wasn't important, and she really was," Jack said. "She was to us."

"Of course she was," Megan said. "But you know, it's kind of true she was ordinary too. She was average height, not fat or thin, the middle child in her family."

"Like Emily?" Thomas suggested. "If you filled in cards like that for her, she'd sound so ordinary, but once you know her like we do, and like Granny knew all of us, you see how special she really is."

That's what Granny had put in Emily's box, the knowledge that however ordinary she was, there were people who loved her and to them she was special.

"That's perfect," Jack said. "But you weren't really worried about being ordinary were you, Emily?"

"No. I was once, but Granny put me right. She asked me if she were ordinary and when I said of course not, she gave me all these to read. I wanted to keep them, but… Oh!"

"What is it, Emily? Something weird?" Chloe asked.

"She joked they were family heirlooms, to be passed on to her descendents."

"Well, you're one of them," Thomas pointed out.

"Not quite." Tears began to pour down Emily's face.

Her cousins got up and either held a hand or hugged her. It helped a little.

"I'm fine, honestly. It's just hormones. You see, I'm not just one descendent, but two. I'm pregnant." She didn't get a chance to tell them of her sorrow that she'd not known quite soon enough to tell Granny. That she'd not spoken of her suspicion, hope, a baby was on the way, rather than waiting to be sure. Waiting until it was too late. Because she'd not told Granny, she'd found it difficult to tell anyone else, except her husband.

There were lots more hugs and warm congratulations.

"I thought you'd put on a bit of weight," Thomas said. "How far along are you?"

"Just long enough to know it will be a girl. We're going to name her Helena, after Granny."

"The first of us to have a baby. That makes you special, Emily," Megan said.

"And it might explain something else," Chloe said. "Is there anything more in that box, Emily?"

There was. A bangle engraved with 'Helena'.

"I noticed it wasn't in my box," Chloe said. "Like Jack said everyone, me included, expected I'd get all Granny's jewellery. But she wanted Emily to have that, so she got me a replacement."

"She knew," Emily said. "She really knew."

24. A Tidy Haunting

Who'd have thought the hardest part of haunting a person would be to get them to notice it was happening?

One difficulty was that, because my unfinished business was with my husband Martin, it was technically only him I was supposed to haunt. That made communicating with his new lady friend complicated.

The second problem was the fact I'd got used to performing only very subtle actions, as initially I hadn't wanted Martin to be aware of my presence. If he thought I was still in this world, in whatever form, he'd search for me, try to be with me and never find happiness with anyone else. In life that's what I'd thought I wanted, but you see things a little differently in death.

Although he has many excellent qualities, Martin is not a tidy man. It was the biggest difference between us. He joked once, "If you ever came back and haunted me, Laura, you'd be the world's tidiest poltergeist."

"I won't do that," I'd promised, "But I'd have something to say to whoever took my place."

"No one could do that."

I'd been pleased then, but of course I didn't know I'd die so young. That I'd be unable to move on, leaving him to face decades being miserable and alone. Just as in life, my happiness in death depended on his.

I'm proud of the tactful way I drew his attention where I wanted it. Gradually I reminded him there were women other than his dead wife and things he could enjoy without her. I'd knocked a pen onto the floor so he'd kneel to retrieve it and notice a colleague's excellent legs. When he'd chucked a pile of junk mail into the bin I'd blown a leaflet from the college off course, giving him another chance to read it.

I let him choose for himself. He didn't opt for Tanya from the office, but Nichola at the local history class I'd nudged him into joining. An excellent choice, I thought.

She liked him. He liked her. Neither of them did anything about it, so I tried to step up my activities. Just as Martin had once joked, I really am a poltergeist. That means I can, to a limited extent, move things in the living world.

Displacing those small, light objects belonging to Martin, was fairly simple once I got the hang of it. Much like, as a toddler, I learned to grasp the chocolate I wanted and guide it into my mouth, or to push unpleasant vegetables off my plate.

Controlling anything larger than a mobile phone, or any object not directly associated with Martin, required a great deal of practise and effort, but it's amazing what you can do if you're sufficiently motivated.

One rainy night when Nichola visited the loo after their evening class I wedged the door shut for a few minutes, so she'd walk out the front of the building as Martin drove by from the car park. Just as she was caught in his headlights I wrenched her umbrella inside out. He stopped to offer her a lift and then, realising he passed her home to reach his, arranged to pick her up and drive her back in future.

I repeated my trick of blowing leaflets about, take away menus this time, to get them to share a meal. Once they had, they began seeing a lot more of each other.

They went out together for a couple of months. Then started staying home together one or two nights a week. Sometimes at his place, more often at hers. It was much tidier and even Martin was beginning to appreciate not having a twenty minute search for every single thing he wanted to use. They were good together and should have shared more than the occasional night, but one thing stood in the way of their happiness – me.

Or rather his memories of me, and the feeling that loving Nichola was be a betrayal of his dead wife, were keeping them from sharing their lives as fully as possible. What could I do?

I'd promised Martin there would be no tidy hauntings for him, and that proved to be binding. Making a mess was, I found, no easier.

Death doesn't change a person very much. I could move a pen or a leaflet so Martin would pick it up and so continue his life, but I couldn't just strew litter for no specific reason. It wouldn't have done any good in any case, as he'd not have known it was me. To be honest, looking at the state of his place I doubted he'd even notice. Nichola would and I'd made no promises to her.

"I hadn't realised how much it bothered me that the painting on the stairs was crooked," she said one day as they climbed up to her flat. "After slipping slightly when I tried to reach it I told myself it didn't matter, but I'm much happier now it's straight."

I liked her all the better for appreciating my efforts, even though it took them both a long time to realise who was behind them.

"Oh, good," Martin said. He didn't realise she thought he'd fixed it and she didn't realise that, despite being a little taller, it was also out of his reach.

Her grateful words about the previous night's washing up being done by morning and coats and shoes put neatly away didn't make him suspect I'd been busy, but they did prompt him to make more of an effort himself.

"I'm sorry I didn't before. Laura used to do all that kind of thing." He dropped his head. "I teased her about it, but never thought to do my share. I wasn't fair to her and I'm not being fair to her memory now. I'm sorry, but I don't think we should see each other any more."

Despite his words, he didn't leave. I was sure he hoped for a sign that he didn't have to, and I wished desperately to provide one, but could think of nothing which might convince him to stay. Looking at Nichola I had no doubt she felt exactly as I did.

After a long moment of silence I hurled myself into the corner of the kitchen where, until very recently, there had been a stack of baking equipment Nichola's gran had given her in the hope she'd make use of it now the older woman no longer did. They couldn't see or hear me, but both of them looked in my direction.

"Where did you put all that stuff?" Nichola asked at the same time as Martin said, "You found a home for your gran's stuff then?"

"I didn't move it," Martin said.

"Neither did I."

"I'm sure it was there this morning."

It was, and neither of them had left the flat and nobody but I had visited.

"One of us must have shifted it without thinking," Martin said, a little doubtfully.

"You remember the crooked painting?" Nichola asked.

"I remember you being pleased it had been straightened."

"You didn't do that?"

"No."

"On my birthday, did you let yourself in and do the laundry and vacuuming before I got home from work?"

"No, I didn't." He took a deep breath and continued quietly, "I think maybe Laura did, even though she promised she wouldn't."

"What do you mean?" Nichola asked.

He told her about his joke that I'd haunt him with tidiness.

"She hasn't, Martin. It's me who's been haunted, if that's what's really happening."

"She said she'd do that… well, she said she'd want a word with whoever took her place."

"It does seem more like she's trying to tell me something than scare me off," the clever young woman replied.

"Like what?"

"I don't know. Maybe we should look for gran's baking tins and stuff. That might be a clue."

"OK."

I don't know when they found them, if they ever did, because they first found other things – signs from me.

Instead of their clothes being on opposite sides of the wardrobe they discovered each of his shirts next to one of her tops, all his trousers alongside her jeans and skirts. His keys which he'd thought were zipped into his jacket pocket sat neatly on the coffee table beside the ones Nichola thought were in her bag.

"I think you're right. Laura is doing this. She's putting all our stuff together."

"Why?" Nichola seemed to be prompting him to work it out, rather than asking something she didn't know.

"Because she wants us to be together."

As he finally understood that, I felt myself float free and drift up and away from the land of the living.

Thank you for reading this book. I hope you enjoyed it. If you did, I'd really appreciate a short review on Amazon, Goodreads – or anywhere else.

To learn more about my writing life, hear about new releases and get a free exclusive ebook, sign up to my newsletter – subscribepage.io/ItLSNa or you can find the link on my website patsycollins.co.uk

<u>More Books by Patsy Collins</u>

Short story collections

Over The Garden Fence
Up The Garden Path
Through The Garden Gate
In The Garden Air
Beyond The Garden Wall

No Family Secrets
Can't Choose Your Family
Keep It In The Family
Family Feeling
Happy Families

Criminal Intent
Crime In Mind

All That Love Stuff
With Love And Kisses
Lots Of Love
Love Is The Answer

Slightly Spooky Stories I
Slightly Spooky Stories II
Slightly Spooky Stories III
Slightly Spooky Stories IV

Just A Job
Perfect Timing
A Way With Words
Dressed To Impress
Coffee & Cake
Making A Move
Days To Remember
Not A Drop To Drink
A Clean Bill Of Health
Your Good Health

Non-fiction

From Story Idea To Reader
(co-written with Rosemary J. Kind)

A Year Of Ideas:
365 sets of writing prompts and exercises

Novels

Firestarter
Escape To The Country
A Year And A Day
Paint Me A Picture
Leave Nothing But Footprints
Acting Like A Killer

Little Mallow cosy mystery series

Disguised Murder and Community Spirit in Little Mallow
Dependable Friends and Deceitful Neighbours
in Little Mallow
Deadly Words and Innocent Gossip in Little Mallow

www.ingramcontent.com/pod-product-compliance
Lightning Source LLC
Chambersburg PA
CBHW070500170726
48291CB00008B/2581